Other Avon Books by
P. M. Carlson

AUDITION FOR MURDER

Murder is Academic

P.M. CARLSON

AVON
PUBLISHERS OF BARD, CAMELOT, DISCUS AND FLARE BOOKS

AVON BOOKS
A division of
The Hearst Corporation
1790 Broadway
New York, New York 10019

Copyright © 1985 by Patricia Carlson
Published by arrangement with the author
Library of Congress Catalog Card Number: 85-90659
ISBN: 0-380-89738-5

First Avon Printing, October 1985

AVON TRADEMARK REG. U. S. PAT. OFF. AND IN OTHER COUNTRIES, MARCA REGISTRADA, HECHO EN U. S. A.

Printed in the U. S. A.

WFH 10 9 8 7 6 5 4 3 2 1

For the Ixil and other victims

'Tis present death I beg: and one thing more,
That womanhood denies my tongue to tell.
O! keep me from their worse than killing lust.

—*Titus Andronicus,* act 2, scene 3

MURDER IS
ACADEMIC

10 Kaoo
(March 6, 1968)

This bitch was unconscious already. He must have clamped too hard on her mouth. When the need was on him he didn't pay much attention. He had an image of the greasy edge of the curtain, the steamy city outside the window. He was six, trying to hide behind the curtain. It smelled like mold and smoke. He kept looking out at the dark hot sidewalk so he wouldn't see the knife in Pa's hand.

He shook his head. No. Now he was in control. He stood up and refastened his belt. This part would be easier anyway: she was so still. He pulled out the knife again and adjusted it carefully, just there on the neck, jugular not carotid. Don't want it spurting. And afterward, carefully, the triangle on the right cheekbone, just like the mark on Mum's cheek. Bitch. She'd never control him now. Wipe the blade, close the knife. Knife and tissue in pocket. Nobody around. Pick up the puppy. Walk casually to the Chevy. Drive away. Carefully.

He tried to remember what she looked like. Young, he thought. Blonde? Well, he could read about her this afternoon. He generally recognized the pictures.

Bitch. She'd had it coming.

"In another set of studies on moral development, Piaget investigated what children thought about lies told by people with different intentions." Professor Davies smiled benignly at the class. Damn, thought Mary Beth, he's going to do it again. Only three minutes to go, and he was starting a new example. "For example, Piaget

11

asked children to compare two cases. In the first, a boy tells his mother he has seen a dog as big as a cow.''

Mary Beth didn't think he meant to run over; he just never checked his watch. The course was interesting enough, a good way for graduate students to satisfy the social science requirement. But it usually made her late to her seminar on Mayan languages. And that was her most important course this term, taught by her thesis adviser. Not wise to offend your thesis adviser, especially if you were as eager to finish as Mary Beth was. But even the ostentatious closing of books and shuffling of impatient feet did not deter Professor Davies. He pushed back red hair from his round forehead and adjusted his notes on the tall Victorian lectern.

''In the second case, another boy falsely tells his mother that he has received a good grade. Then Piaget asked the children which lie was worse.''

Mary Beth wrote, ''Which lie is worse?'' and sighed. What was today? 10 Kaoo. The day of the Guardian of the World, not a bad day, usually. But this morning her tall new housemate Maggie, as disgustingly wide awake as the birds outside, had knocked on her door calling, ''Eight o'clock, Mary Beth.'' Shocked, Mary Beth had looked accusingly at her alarm clock, set for seven-thirty.

The clock hadn't been there.

She had hurried to the bathroom crossly, asking Maggie, ''Where's my clock? Someone's run off with my clock!'' But Maggie, munching her toast, had just shaken her black curls, and there hadn't been time to investigate.

''The youngest children focused on the amount of discrepancy from real life. Boys do get good grades sometimes, the children reasoned, so *that* lie wasn't far from the truth. However, dogs are never as big as cows, so that lie was worse. At this stage of moral development, intentions don't count.''

The phrase echoed in Mary Beth's ears. Intentions don't count, Tip had said; how could you do this to me? Oh God. A cold panic lapped about her, welling up like icy lava from the underworld. Far in the background, Hun-Came and Vucub-Came began to shriek with silent laughter. Willing them away, she clenched the pen in her fist until she could feel bruising pain against her finger joints. She looked around, frantic for support, for reality. The big old paneled lecture hall, worn floor, crooked brown stain in the corner of the ceiling. Okay. That was real. That was now. The rows of impatient students. Professor Davies, pudgy and red-haired. Piaget's

12

theories. Okay, she told herself fiercely, everything is okay. She stole a glance at Maggie, slouching serenely next to her, long legs stretched well under the seat in front. Everything was okay.

Mary Beth held them at bay and slowly they retreated—Hun-Came and Vucub-Came, the Lords of Death. Slowly the lapping terror ebbed. She concentrated on her feet, her ankles, her knees, working her way up her body and consciously relaxing each part, but she could still feel her rushing pulse and the chill perspiration on her skin, and the shame. She had to finish soon. Get away from here, get back to Guatemala, try to find the bright and confident Mary Beth she had once been.

". . . a stage that takes motivation into account," Professor Davies was saying. "These older children claim that exaggerating the size of the dog is okay, because there's no . . ."

Somewhere near at hand a bell shrilled. Startled, Mary Beth looked around. Professor Davies hesitated, then went on, raising his voice a little.

". . . no danger that the mother will believe . . ."

Another bell, deeper than the first, joined in from across the room. And in another second, another bell, from the back, with an awful familiarity. Oh Jesus. Maggie! Mary Beth turned accusingly to her friend. Calm and amused, Maggie's blue eyes met hers for an instant and then looked back at Professor Davies. More bells were joining in, eight or ten by now. Professor Davies, bewildered, turned his head back and forth, surveying the old hall in perplexity. Radiators, venetian blinds, wastebaskets, paneling, every nook and crevice seemed to be ringing. Finally the answer struck him. He looked at his watch.

"Oh my." Mary Beth could not hear him above the shrill cacophony, but saw his lips form the words. He stared at the watch a moment and a grudging smile twisted his mouth. He closed his notebook and shrugged elaborately at the class. Relieved, the students laughed and applauded as he left.

Mary Beth tossed her books into her big Guatemalan bag and stood up, still a little shaky but in control again. She marched up the sloping aisle to the back entry stairwell. There was her missing clock—in the cranny where the banister joined the wall. She silenced it and carried it back down the side aisle to her friend.

Maggie handed her a brown paper sack. "It'll travel better in this," she said warily. She was a little uneasy; they hadn't known each other long. Mary Beth took the sack and followed her. Maggie was making an efficient orbit around the room, pulling alarm clocks from behind radiators and wastebaskets. Other students, grinning, congratulated her on their way out.

Mary Beth said, "Maggie, you're some kind of a loon."

"Do you realize that you may even be on time to your seminar if you leave now?"

"No need to get prickly." Mary Beth dropped her bagged clock into her bookbag and grinned at Maggie. "I won't evict you."

Maggie, a hint of relief shining in the deep blue eyes, smiled back. "My lucky day," she said airily.

"We Mayan landlords are very conscious of time," said Mary Beth, putting on a landlord face. "It was a good cause. Shows highly developed morality. See you later, loon." She swung her bookbag over her shoulder and went out into the March cold to class.

The letter was waiting in the box marked Freeman, tossed in casually by a bored secretary. Jane glanced at the return address and tucked the envelope hastily into her briefcase, then headed for privacy. Maybe her own little experimental room, down in the basement. But when she arrived she saw that the big equipment room next door was empty too, and so she went in there instead, because she never felt easy in small rooms.

The letter was from the *Verbal Learning Quarterly*. She slit it open neatly with her letter-knife, glanced at the brief paragraph, breathed "Wow!" to a nearby tachistoscope, and began to skip around the room.

"Hey, you got a nice high," said Josh Hinshaw admiringly from the door. Jane turned and grinned at him. She must have looked silly, bouncing around in her dignified gray suit and high-heeled pumps. Such actions were more suited to the embroidered jeans and bright beads that Josh wore. Well, she always had been too impulsive.

"Just got an article accepted," she informed him.

"Hey, good for you." Josh ambled in and sat on his desk. "Is it about these babies we're testing?"

"God, no! We're miles from publishing anything on them. This article was finished a long time ago. But it's a relief to get it into print."

"Yeah."

"Listen, I'm going up to grab a cup of coffee." The news was

14

good; she could face her colleagues. "But we have two babies coming in this afternoon, so I'll see you soon."

"Okay. Three-thirty?"

"Right. See you then. Cheers!"

Jane paused in the women's room to be sure that her long brown hair, braided and wrapped neatly around her head, had not jounced loose during her little dance of triumph. Then, still tingling with pleasure at the joyful news, she headed up the solid staircase of the paneled thirties building to the faculty lounge on the main psychology floor. Today's paper was lying on the coffee table. She got herself a cup of coffee and glanced down at the front page. The headlines spoke of more gore in Vietnam. And the Triangle Murderer had apparently struck again in nearby Syracuse. Four victims so far. She reached down for the paper.

"They did what?"

Jane straightened as Linc Berryman and Dick Davies came into the faculty lounge. Linc sounded even more excited than usual.

"They had dozens of alarm clocks," Dick was saying, "all set for two-fifteen." His pudgy face was rueful. "I never heard anything like it!"

"Good Lord!" Linc had a booming laugh. A tall, muscular young man with a bushy beard, he specialized in biopsychology, and had given guest lectures for Jane a time or two. Linc went over well with students, since he was so clearly convinced that birdsong was among the most fascinating topics known to the human mind. He was up for a tenure decision this year too.

"What's the joke?" asked Jane.

"My disorganized ways finally caught up with me," explained Dick. "I always have trouble stopping on time. Today my twelve o'clock students hid dozens of alarm clocks around the room, all set for the end of the period. Incredible sound!"

Jane laughed. "What did you do?"

"What could I do? I quit. Right in midsentence." He made a face of comic defeat.

She shook her head, smiling, and took a sip of coffee. Poor Dick. He was notorious at faculty meetings too for having no sense of time. Jane paid careful attention to Dick and his moods these days, as she did to all tenured professors. Dick was something of an enigma, a social psychologist who knew all the right words to say about equality for blacks and women, but still tended to be abrupt and impatient with her and with the two other women professors at faculty meetings. He'd been raised in working-class Baltimore, he'd said; old attitudes died hard, even if you were an expert in attitude change. But Dick's work was undeniably good. She had been on a couple of committees for his students' theses and was impressed by the sharp mind he brought to bear on their research. He had received tenure two years ago. Eleven articles, three of them quite influential, a couple of book chapters, and a book in manuscript.

For Jane, today's acceptance made nine articles. At the moment her own book was just an outline and a preliminary list of references.

"Was the whole class involved?" she asked.

"I got the impression most of them were as surprised as I was," said Dick.

"You're right," said a new voice. They all turned to the door. A woman student stood there. Tall, with a pleasant smile, feathery black curls, vivid blue eyes.

"Hi, Maggie. You know something about this episode?" asked Dick.

"I wanted to confess before you started blaming anyone else. Piaget would be ashamed of me if I intended to deceive."

Dick smiled. "I see. You're afraid I'll have the whole class write 'I will not set alarm clocks in social psych' one thousand times?"

"Well, I'm new here. For all I know, the rack and thumbscrews are still in use."

"We reserve those for nontenured professors," said Dick with a sly glance at Jane and Linc. They laughed dutifully. He turned back to Maggie. "But I got the message." For the first time Jane caught the undertone of anger in his cheerful voice.

"It was a bit Pavlovian, though," Jane chided Maggie.

"Yes. A crude, old-fashioned approach," said Maggie apologetically. "Not really worthy of this high-technology department. But the situation didn't seem to call for a full-scale sit-in."

"Thank God for that," said Dick. He looked Maggie over, and said the right thing. "Well, I'll try to reform."

"Okay. So will I," she promised.

"Want to come in and have some genuine faculty instant coffee to seal the truce?" he offered.

"Thanks." She gave him a broad bright smile and hefted her clanking bookbag. "But I've got a lot of alarm clocks to return now. Some people didn't exactly know they were loaning them. I have to get them back before I flunk moral development."

Linc frowned after her. "Handsome woman. Who is she?"

"Maggie Ryan," said Dick. "New grad in statistics."

"Working with Walt Bennett?"

"And with people in the math department. Walt says she's got more math background than psych, so he put her in my course to fill her in. Blast him."

"Never trust a number cruncher," said Linc. He sat down on the sofa and looked up at Jane. "How are you doing?"

"Fine," she said casually. "Just got an article accepted by the *Verbal Learning Quarterly*. The one on negation."

"Terrific! That's a good journal."

Dick asked, "And how is your project with babies?"

"Slow. I worked it out. By the time you make allowances for missed appointments, we test an average of point seven babies per day, working at full speed."

"This study will be included in your book, right?" asked Linc.

"Chapter Four. I hope so," said Jane fervently. She hated the suspense of waiting for the results that would tell her if she was on the right track.

"Best not to count chickens," said Dick, sitting next to Linc and picking up the paper. He was smiling, but Jane felt the sharp and icy edge in his comment. Or was it her imagination? She touched her briefcase where the letter lay and, comforted, turned to Linc.

"How are you doing?" she asked.

"I've got two articles out to journals," he replied. "One on nesting, one on heredity. Haven't heard about either of them."

"Good luck." Jane was sincere. Her relationship with Linc Berryman and Hal Hazlitt was odd this year. Theoretically, Dick and the rest of the tenured faculty could choose to vote tenure for all three candidates, or for none. As a practical matter, though, she knew they were rivals; any one of them clearly behind or ahead of the others could affect the vote for all three. But despite the competition, there was comradeship too. They all knew the hopes and fears that accompanied the mailing of articles to journals, brief summaries of months of work. It was a little like being baseball players on a farm team, she thought; they simultaneously worked together, helping each other, and competed against each other for the call to the big leagues.

Which would never come if she spent all her time talking. She said, "Well, folks, back to work. I'll see you later. Cheers!"

"See you, Jane."

As she walked down the wainscoted hall to her office, Jane pulled out her appointment book. Two babies this afternoon, one at three-thirty and one at five-thirty. Josh would help her run the machines, as usual, but Jane alone would meet the mothers, who felt more comfortable if she wired up the babies. Josh was too much a flower child, with too much frizzy hair and too many beads, to inspire confidence. Jane, on the other hand, looked both kind and scientific; she seemed to make the mothers feel confident that no stray jolts of electricity would be allowed to course through their infants. In fact, the power all came from the equipment room next door, where Josh presided. Of course, it couldn't reach the baby. But there was a lot of voltage in there, and it was best to keep the mothers uninformed and reassured.

As Jane approached her office door, she saw a knot of students huddled over a newspaper. She recognized a couple of her own students—Jackie Edwards and Terry Poole. And Maggie Ryan was there, the bag of alarm clocks on the floor beside her. "What's happening?" Jane asked.

"Did you see this about Christie James?" asked Jackie, her dark eyes perturbed.

"Christie James?"

"In the education school here," said Maggie. "She's the one the Triangle Murderer just killed."

"My God! One of our students? I haven't read it yet!"

"Yeah. It was only ten or fifteen miles from here. She was on her way back from Syracuse after a visit home."

"Professor Freeman, can't we do anything?" Terry Poole was vivacious, black, intelligent, usually smiling but today very grim.

"You mean for a memorial?"

"Hell, no!" said Maggie. "We want to find out how to stop guys like that. Why do they do it? How can we fight back?"

"Right!" agreed Terry. "This is just the last straw. Vietnam and assassinations and riots, maybe we can't do anything about those. But why the hell can't we stop just one flaky dude?"

"Okay," said Jane. The group was determined and angry and young, and something in her responded. One flaky dude. At least wrest control from him. "I don't know what we can do either, but we can get together and find out."

18

"How?" asked Terry.

"We're smart, we'll figure it out. Terry, you're first lieutenant. I'll use my so-called elite status as professor to enlist people to help—karate experts or policemen or whatever we decide we need. You take care of the details, okay?"

"Terrific!"

"For starts, run off some flyers. We'll meet Saturday at two o'clock. Get my secretary to find us a room. And we'll talk then about what we need to find out."

"Great!" said Terry. "What should I call it? Rape group?"

"Only if you want to attract every lamebrained male humorist on campus," said Maggie.

"Women Against Rape," said Jane, feeling militant. "WAR."

"Hey, right! Thanks, Professor Freeman!"

"Glad to help," said Jane. "Well, cheers."

She left the group chattering more hopefully and thought how resilient humans were—to live in such a world and still want to associate with each other. How resilient, and how stupid. Especially one named Jane Freeman, who had no time to spare now, who should be collecting and analyzing data, finishing the tenure dossier. If this current study came out well statistically, she could include it in the dossier, even if it was not yet accepted by a journal. And that's what she should be working on, her book, her articles, not taking on another time-consuming project. You're as bad as your dad was, she could hear her mother saying. Leap before you look. Wouldn't she ever learn?

But some impulses worked out well. And maybe, just maybe, this group would give someone an extra bit of knowledge to help in a crisis, enable her to come out of it alive instead of dead, like poor Christie James.

Oh, sure. Jane Freeman, savior of the world. If she wanted to save human lives, she'd do better donating to the Red Cross.

She sighed, checked her book again. Before meeting the babies today, she had quizzes to grade from her introductory course, and a new issue of *Acoustics* to read, and four goddamn letters of recommendation. She unlocked her office and glanced with maternal pride at the bookshelf with the eight neat stacks of offprints of her articles. Eight, soon to be nine. She propped the door open and sat down resolutely to work on the first of the letters.

II

10 Hunaapu
(January 27, 1968)

They'd met at the end of January, that terrible January. Mary Beth had been running. Leaden aching legs, gasping lungs seared by chilly air ripping in and out, stringy hair whipping her face, feet thudding, measuring her too-slow progress toward death. And then the little miracle happened. For the first time in weeks, it happened. She felt the pain and depression sliding away, her legs lightening, her lungs expanding. Once again she became Mary Beth Nelson, the Speeding Swede, letterwoman, Phi Beta Kappa. Once again she became the Mary Beth who had driven thousands of miles alone through Mexico and spent six months in a remote and primitive village. High above, in the pale cold northern sky, Hunaapu smiled down at her. Hunaapu, the Sun God, the twin, the hero who had overcome the Lords of Death. Today was his day.

It was seven miles around the golf course, hard frozen miles, a few patches of snow still on the north slopes. She checked her stopwatch at the seven-mile mark. Great. A good run. She jogged back to the gym for her shower with a sense of well-being she'd thought might never return, her body worn and delighted from the good workout. It was Hunaapu's day.

During semester break the gym was almost deserted, eerily vacant. She had her hand on the big gray door to the locker room stairs when she heard, faintly, the sound of a flute. She paused, puzzled. Mozart? Here? And proficiently played. She crossed the hall and opened the door to the basketball court. The sound was coming from high in the bleachers, echoing a bit in the vast hall.

20

Mary Beth untied the sweatshirt from her waist, pulled it on, and climbed up the bleachers. Here the acoustics were better. The woman flutist glanced up and then gazed into space as she continued the piece. Nice tone. A blue sweatband held back her black curls. The music wound up and down, sweet and controlled, and came to its foreordained and perfect conclusion. Mary Beth watched her take the flute in one hand and lean forward a little to perch her elbows on the back of the seat in front of her. She returned Mary Beth's look of good-natured appraisal.

"Hey," blurted Mary Beth, "you're really very good."

"Thank you. Glad to meet a fellow spirit. *Anima sana in corpore sano.*"

Mary Beth pushed a strand of blonde hair from her eyes. "Not so much healthy as thirsty, right now."

"In soul or in body?"

"Maybe both." Jesus, what am I saying, thought Mary Beth, suddenly embarrassed.

"Me too." The flutist stood up and added pragmatically, "Let's go get a Coke. I'm Maggie Ryan."

"Mary Beth Nelson."

"What instrument do you play?"

"Bassoon. Hey, listen, we have the start of a woodwind quintet. We need a flute. Also a clarinet."

Maggie was dismantling and cleaning the flute and placing it in its case. "Okay," she said readily. "I'd like that. I hate violins."

"Good. I mean, good that you'll work with us."

"It sounds like fun. Where are the Coke machines?"

"Downstairs, outside the locker room door. Are you new here?"

"Just arrived. What's your sport, Mary Beth?"

"Cross-country."

"I'm a gymnast."

"Oh." Mary Beth noticed as they descended the bleachers that bars and beams had been set up on the floor around the basketball court. All the same, she was a little surprised. Maggie was even taller than she was, rangy—not the usual short compact gymnast's build.

"Recreational," explained Maggie, reading her look. "They don't let grads on the teams here anyway, do they?"

"No. I've got the same problem."

"Keep it up anyway. *Corpore sano.*"

"Right." Mary Beth smiled. They bought Cokes and started toward the women's lockers again. "You'd better give me your address and phone so I can call you when we get the quintet organized."

"I don't know it yet myself. That's one thing I'm doing today. Looking for a room."

Mary Beth hesitated only an instant. She didn't know a thing about this musical gymnast, really. But it was Hunaapu, a favorable day. She said, "We've got one. Seventy-five a month."

"Complete with quintet?"

Mary Beth laughed. "Sorry. Bassoon and horn only, so far. The oboe lives a block and a half from us."

"Is your place far from campus?"

"Fifteen-minute walk."

"How many people?"

"You'd be the fourth. Your own room, share the rest of the house. Walton Street."

Their lockers were not very close together, and they had to raise their voices as they stripped and showered.

"Does the non–quintet person play rock all night?"

"Jackie? No. She's quiet. Claims to be nonmusical, but she likes to listen. It's quiet, really. A haven. I was there last year, and away this fall, and just got back. It's nice."

"I'd like to have a look at your haven, Mary Beth."

"Great! Can you come over now? I'm going home for lunch."

"Okay." And after a moment, "What are you studying?"

"Linguistics."

"Any special language?"

"Spanish to earn my keep. Ixil for love."

"Ee-sheel?"

"Yes. Spelled I-X-I-L. A Mayan language."

"Mayan!" Dark curls dripping, Maggie appeared suddenly, wrapped in a towel, by Mary Beth's shower. The quick blue eyes took in the red scab and the fading bruises on Mary Beth's ribs and hips before she could hide. She turned abruptly away and shut off the water. But Maggie's voice did not falter. "That's wonderful. But I thought their culture was pretty much extinct."

"There are only fragments left. It's sad," said Mary Beth, grabbing her own towel and covering up. "The Spaniards wiped out all they could. You know, for religion. Gold and religion. But

22

some Mayan religious traditions are still practiced quietly. And some languages are still around.''

''Religious traditions? Aren't they Catholic by now?''

''Well, they avoid trouble by saying so. They put the Catholic names on Mayan gods. There's Kubaal Qii, the Creator of Humanity, who was killed by his jealous brothers and rose on the third day. He's also called Jesus. Kuchuch, the female deity, is also called Mary.''

''I see.'' Maggie was back at her own locker. ''Keep the god but change the label.''

''Yeah. The lesser gods have saints' names too. The Ixil celebrate the saints' days, but they also keep track of the Mayan year and the Mayan holy year, and celebrate those too. And that's no small feat. The calendar is complicated.''

''I've heard of the Mayan calendar. Also that they invented zero. Do the Ixil have that too?''

''No. That was part of the ancient writing system. Wiped out. The Ixil today are mostly illiterate, so they can't use zero. I think it's even more amazing, because they keep the count in their heads.''

''Impressive people.''

''They have stories,'' said Mary Beth, splashing on cologne. They were dressed now, shirts and jeans and jackets and bookbags, the indigenous costume of North American young adulthood. They pushed open the door. ''There's an elaborate underworld filled with gods of death and other horrible things. One story is about two miraculous boys, the Heroic Twins, Hunaapu and Xbelenque. They want to avenge their father and uncle, who were taken by the Lords of Death. So they go down to the underworld. The twins are clever.'' Mary Beth stopped at the junction of the halls and said anxiously, ''Let's go out the front way.''

Maggie was already halfway to the back exit, closer, a white metal door with a round steel knob. ''Oh, I thought Walton Street was this direction.''

''Yes, but . . .'' In the back of Mary Beth's mind, Hun-Came and Vucub-Came stirred, began to wake, grinning the grin of death. She turned away. ''Please, let's go this way.''

Maggie, obeying, asked, ''So what did these clever twins do?''

''Well, knowing someone's name gives you power over him. The twins gain the advantage early by learning the names of the Lords of Death, Hun-Came and Vucub-Came, and all their under-

23

lings. The twins are put through many trials. There's a red-hot bench, and a cave full of vampire bats, and one of ice. There's a river of blood, and . . .'' Mary Beth felt herself growing cold. Oh Jesus. She clenched her hands and forced herself on. ''And there's a room full of sacrificial knives. Hun-Came and Vucub-Came overcome the twins eventually, but the boys come back to life and disguise themselves as sword dancers. The Lords of Death watch the twins dancing and chopping each other apart with swords, and then miraculously making themselves whole again.'' The cold wave was retreating. ''And the Lords of Death like the trick so much they want to do it too. So the twins oblige and chop them apart. But of course they don't bring them back to life.''

''Smart.''

''Yes. They eventually take over the sun and moon, and light the world.''

''Because they knew the names of the gods. Hun-Came?''

''And Vucub-Came.''

''I see.''

''The old stories don't die. Every day the Sun God makes the same journey the twins made. It's swallowed by death in the west, and goes to the deepest level of the underworld, and then climbs out again, reborn in the east. Then it rises to the highest heaven and eventually sinks to death again. The days are gods too.''

''Really?''

''Today is Hunaapu's day.''

''One of the twins.''

''Yes. It's supposed to be a favorable day.''

''And tomorrow?''

''Imush, the Earth God. And then Iiq, the Wind God. And then . . .'' Mary Beth covered her face with her hand. Oh God, oh God, what was to become of her? She couldn't even carry on a normal conversation. Maggie was watching her, concerned. She forced herself to continue. ''The day names repeat every twenty days. There's also a cycle of thirteen day numbers. Numbers are gods too.''

''Hell, I knew that already,'' said Maggie, helping her out.

''You did?''

''I'm a statistician.''

''Oh God. Why?''

Maggie smiled. ''Accident, partly. I've always liked math. For several reasons I wanted to clear out of my undergraduate college early, and a math major was the most efficient way. But a couple of months ago I found myself homesick for all the messy human things in the arts and social sciences, and I figured statistics would be a bridge. Math applied to human problems.''

"I've never liked math," said Mary Beth dubiously.

"Yeah, a lot of people don't. But I find it very aesthetic. Pure and formal, beautiful and divorced from reality. Except that it isn't. Somehow it lets us describe the universe in nonsensical ways that are truer than the commonsense ways.''

"I see. You would've made a good Maya.''

Maggie's delighted grin was very wide. "Hey, that's my favorite compliment this month!''

The house on Walton Street was post–World War I: massive square brick with a full-width porch with thick columns; capacious living room, dining room, and kitchen downstairs; four corner bedrooms and a bathroom upstairs. They went in the front door. Sue, broad and freckled, was back in the kitchen fixing herself a tuna sandwich.

"Greetings!" she bellowed enthusiastically. "Who's this?''

Mary Beth performed the introductions. "Maggie Ryan, Sue Snyder.''

"Hi, Sue. You must be the French horn," said Maggie.

"Fat, loud, and essential," agreed Sue. "That's me. And you?''

Maggie smiled. "Long and fond of heights.''

Mary Beth laughed. Sue thought an instant, then beamed. "A flute! You found a flute, Mary Beth!''

"She's a gymnast too.''

"Ha!" Sue's laugh was like a bark. Mary Beth liked her, but just now she found herself wishing that she would be more restrained. Somehow already she desperately wanted Maggie to stay with them. Sue was a little rowdy for some tastes.

Mary Beth said warningly, "Hey, listen. She also wants to look at the room.''

Sue shut up abruptly and surveyed the rangy, dark-haired visitor more critically. "Hmm," she said. "That requires thought. The flute is a plus, but we don't really need a gymnast.''

"I swim and bicycle and repair cars too," said Maggie. "My faults include forgetting to make my bed and an unfortunate interest in statistics.''

"Dear me, numbers. That is a drawback," said Sue reflectively.

25

"Mary Beth is a calendar freak, of course. But Jackie's in French literature and I'm in Russian. Would we be able to communicate?"

"En français, peut-être. Mais je ne parle pas russe."

Sue, startled by the flawless accent, bounced right back. *"D'accord.* That will do. Also, we're very studious here."

"I just finished twenty-one hours last term, mostly advanced math. And I promise to indulge in my noisier dissipations away from home."

"A dissipated statistician. God," said Sue, pleased. "What's your religion?"

"Let's say Pythagorean."

"Ah. Math and music, right? Celestial spheres. That's okay: we'll take anyone who doesn't distribute leaflets. Finances?"

"The usual monthly pittance. Teaching assistantship."

"Okay. One other thing. As for the opposite sex . . ."

Even Sue couldn't ignore the warning flash in Maggie's eyes or the sudden icy edge in her voice. "Yes?"

"Oh, nothing. I just wanted to say that guys are allowed for dinner if it's okay with whoever's cooking. But nothing rowdy. And nothing stronger than pot on the premises."

"Strict hours and chaste habits. It's a goddamn nunnery," said Maggie. But she and Sue were smiling at each other again.

"Okay," roared Sue enthusiastically. "Let's take her, Mary Beth!"

"Just a minute," said Maggie.

"What? Qualms already?"

"No, a couple of questions. First, is the house okay? Heat, running water, and so forth?"

"No problems. Upstairs shower goes cold if some dummy turns on the kitchen sink faucet, that's all."

"I see. And is there anything I ought to know about you?"

"Well, as you can see, I'm just about perfect," admitted Sue modestly. "The Speeding Swede here smells too good since she came back from the Tropics, but she's still basically a good sort. And Jackie . . ."

"Jackie has a reputation for being quiet, but that's only in comparison to Sue," said Jackie. She and her friend Peter had appeared at the kitchen door, his wiry arm around her shoulders.

"Oh, hi, Jackie. Hi, Peter. This is Maggie Ryan. May rent the room. Plays flute."

26

"Really? I'm the oboe!" said Peter. "Now all we need is a clarinet!"

"She's also a statistician," warned Sue, as though announcing that she carried typhoid.

"But I overheard some authentic French too." Jackie had shiny dark hair and a warm smile. She held out her hand to Maggie. *"Enchantée."*

"So here we all are!" said Sue expansively. "Any other questions, Maggie?"

"One teeny thing. May I see the room?"

Sue guffawed. "Suspicious bitch, ain't she? Take her up, Swede."

Mary Beth led the way through the dining room and living room. An old sofa was covered with a Guatemalan blanket, the oak mantel displayed some French pottery and a Russian doll, the hearth held a basket of split firewood. They climbed the stairs to the big northeast room that overlooked the street. Maggie checked the closet and the desk, then sat on the stripped bed and looked thoughtfully out the window. It did seem monastic, thought Mary Beth, seeing the bare white room through a stranger's eyes. Outside, through a tangle of winter-naked branches like a grill across the windows, the university and town stood gray against the blue sky. Mary Beth waited a moment, then sat on the bed next to her.

"What do you think?" she asked anxiously.

For an instant, as she watched Maggie call back her thoughts from some melancholy place, she felt the same closeness she had sensed in the bleachers. Two parched souls.

"Your nunnery is exactly what I need," said Maggie softly, still looking out the window. "A place to start over. To rebuild." Then the blue eyes, direct and disturbing, switched to Mary Beth. "I think for both of us."

III

4 Kamel
(March 13, 1968)

This one was old; wrinkled skin, frail bones. Older even than Mum's mother. The murderer could see Mum, almost, could smell the stench of alcohol with the sharp senses of the eight-year-old. She was begging Pa to stop. Pa had the puppy. Pa was in control. No. No, that was over. Now he was in control himself. He stifled the scream, a feeble scream anyway. She didn't close her eyes, just glared at him. But she wasn't strong either. Old bitch. Trying to control him. The only problem was afterward; he had a little trouble making the triangle neat, because of the softness of the wrinkled skin.

Then he drove away. He dumped the sleepy kitten near the animal shelter.

It wasn't until much later that he noticed a button missing from his shirt.

Terry said, "The victims have all been driving alone on highways around Syracuse. Even Christie James was away from the university, on the way back from visiting her parents."

"How close to Syracuse?" asked Jane. They were sitting in an unused seminar room, desks pushed into a rough circle.

"Closer than this. Fifteen miles away was the farthest, I think."

"That's still too close for comfort," said dark-eyed Monica.

"Yes," Terry agreed. "Let's see. The reports also mention that the victims seem to be suffocated or partly suffocated by a hand

28

across the mouth and nose, and then their throats cut with something that could be just a pocketknife.''

"Okay. We knew that."

"But that's all I could find. The only other thing is the triangle."

"Why do they stop for him? You said their cars were okay."

Terry shrugged. "Nobody knows. Nobody alive."

"Maybe he's got a police uniform or something," suggested Maggie. "I'd stop for a uniform."

"If so, nobody's noticed it yet."

"Nobody alive," said Jane. "Well, keep us posted on developments. I'll see if we can find a policeman on that case to talk to us. And everyone be careful driving around Syracuse. Okay, Jackie, you were going to look up some general precautions."

"Yes," said Jackie. "But you know, if you take all this advice, you can hardly live at all. They say don't go out at night, don't go anywhere alone, keep all your doors and windows locked with deadbolts, don't go into lonely areas. I mean, who wants a life when you can't even go do the laundry?"

"A woman's place is in the home," suggested Sue mockingly.

"Well, the advice is probably good up to a point," said Jane. "But you're right, Jackie. We're all building careers. We have to compete with men. And men go to the library or to the lab at night, whether or not anyone else will go with them. Science would slow to half speed if we all followed those rules."

Monica said, "And a lot of us will end up fending for ourselves and maybe for dependents too, all alone. We really have to take that for a starting point. If life forces us to take risks, how do we minimize them?"

"Okay," said Jane. "Let's look at self-defense, then. Someone recommended a Syracuse man named Ed Hamlin. Maybe we can hire him for a couple of demonstrations."

"Good," said Maggie. "And after that maybe we can talk to a policeman, and a lawyer, to find out what kind of help we can get from them."

"And maybe a bartender or bouncer," suggested Sue. "Someone used to dealing with guys who are out of control."

Jane was writing it all down. "Fine. I'll make some calls. Terry, check back with me at midweek. Right now, I'm afraid I have to go meet a baby."

Gently, Jane rubbed salve into the infant's skin and attached the third electrode carefully, just under the tiny nipple, then pulled down the soft shirt so the baby wouldn't pull away the wires. She gave it a biscuit. It stared, large eyes crossing stupidly at the biscuit clutched at the end of its own short arm, and drooled a little as it pulled it jerkily to its mouth. Jane pressed the switch and the noises began. "Ba-ba-ba-ba-ba." In the next room, faithful needles bobbled on the moving roll of graph paper, recording the sturdy little heartbeat with red lines. The infant listened to the ba-ba-ba for a while and then began to chew on the biscuit. Jane depressed a button, and one of the needles recorded the fact that the subject was eating. The ba-ba-ba series changed to pa-pa-pa. In a moment the subject dropped the biscuit onto the table and began to kick. Jane hit the off button, handed the child its gluey biscuit again, and tenderly removed the electrodes. She swabbed the rosy skin clean.

"Wonderful!" she said to the proud mother. She always told mothers that their infants were wonderful, even perfect. Even when they cried a lot. This one had been okay.

"Did you get what you wanted?" asked the mother anxiously.

"Yes. He was just perfect," Jane said.

"Did Greg understand that tape, do you think?"

"Well, we aren't checking for meaningful words, of course." This mother was a faculty wife, Jane noted; she'd have to explain. "It'll be another six months to a year before Greg starts using words. But he has to know an awful lot before he reaches that stage. And one of the important things is to know at least some of the differences in sounds that are important in English."

"Ba and pa?" asked Greg's mother dubiously. "Those aren't words."

"Right. But if he can't hear the difference between 'bat' and 'pat,' 'bird' and 'purred,' 'bony' and 'pony,' then he can't hear that you're using those different words for different ideas and objects."

"But how can you tell what he can hear, if he can't talk?"

"You're right. That's the hardest thing about working with babies. They can't answer questions about whether two things sound the same or different. But the heart rate changes slightly when a child's attention is caught, so we're measuring that. We play the ba-ba-ba's until he habituates. That means he gets bored. Then we shift to the pa-pa-pa's. If he can't tell the difference yet, there shouldn't be any change in heart rate. He'll still be bored. But if the shift catches his attention, then the heart rate should change a little.''

"I see. That's clever. And what's that salve you put on?''

"Same thing a doctor uses for electrocardiograms. It reduces the skin resistance to an electrical current so we can record the tiny little electrical impulses from his heart.''

"It must be very difficult work.''

"Yes. With children this young, we have to work in roundabout ways. But it's interesting. I'm convinced that they know quite a lot they can't tell us about yet.''

"Oh, yes!'' agreed Greg's mother eagerly. "Greg is a really smart baby. My friend came to visit and he looked at her and said 'Bet' just as clear as day. And her name is Betty! He must have heard us talking to her.''

"Would you like to see a heart rate record?'' asked Jane, stemming what threatened to become a flood of scientifically useless anecdotes about Greg's mental prowess. Mother love, though wonderful for both parties involved, was not very objective. She pulled her sample spool of paper from the counter and showed the mother the red lines. Eventually Greg dropped the damp biscuit again and began to complain, so Jane sent mother and child off, paid with a couple of dollars, the biscuit, and warm thanks for their contribution to the great march of science.

Unbuttoning her lab coat, Jane went thankfully into the big equipment room next door. She was always glad to leave the tiny experimental room, its walls so close around her. For soundproofing reasons she couldn't leave the door open the way she did her office door. It got on her nerves.

"How's it going?'' she asked Josh.

"Fine.'' He had labeled the new record with Greg's age, sex, and the date, and, beads jangling, was putting it away in the cabinet over his desk. Josh preferred to keep his desk right in the equipment room. It was a large room by basement standards and was crowded with scientific equipment—amplifiers, tape recorders, tachistoscopes, polygraphs such as the one Jane was using, and more. A large metal scaffold had been set up across most of the room, with high shelves fixed to it for some of the overflow equipment. The department chairman was trying to locate space for equipment storage, but it was difficult to find in this overcrowded university.

Josh added, "The only problem is that he didn't habituate much."

"Hell!" The trouble with babies was that they came in all speeds. Some of them became bored too quickly and began to fuss. Others, like little Greg, remained interested for too long. In both cases, there was no way to tell from the heart rate records if the babies had noticed the changes in the taped sounds or not. Jane added, "Wish we could screen them first for habituation time."

"Hey, wow!" Josh wore his fuzzy black hair in a ponytail, stored a few dubious substances among the pliers and transistors in his desk, and was often high; but still he managed to keep what he called a good head for machines. He was enthusiastic now about screening the babies. "We could bring them in one day for a pretest, and test them the next with a tape with a tailor-made habituation time. Long, short, or medium."

"Mm." But it took as long to find willing mothers and schedule the babies as it did to think up the logic of the research and make the tapes. Longer. Occasionally Jane wondered why she hadn't gone into some exciting field. Grocery checkouts. Government file clerk. "It would be hard to get them to come twice," she said. "Let's finish this batch. Then if we fail miserably we'll try the other route."

"Okay. But I think it would work better."

"Yes, it probably would. Thanks, Josh."

"Sure."

"Cheers!" Jane hung the lab coat on a peg and started back upstairs to her office. It was past time for cocktails; Greg's mother had wanted to come late. One's life was at the mercy of one's subjects. And of one's journal editors. And especially of one's tenured colleagues. How many hours had she spent on this little study now? Too depressing to count.

"Hi, Jane."

She turned by her own door. "Oh, hi, Linc. How's it going?"

"Fair. I got my nesting paper back from the journal. No go."

"Oh dear."

"Well, it isn't all bad. One of the readers said it would be publishable if I added an additional study to clarify one of the subsidiary points. The editor agrees."

"Will it be hard to do?"

"No. Except that the damn birds won't be ready to nest again for two months." His usual enthusiasm was dimmed today.

Jane said sympathetically, "I was just thinking how much our lives are controlled by our subjects."

"How true." Linc smiled sadly. "Anyway, enough of my troubles. I wanted to ask you a favor."

"Sure. What is it?"

"A girl in my class has come in to see me a couple of times. Very bright, but she says she's in conflict about going into the field professionally. Doesn't know if she wants to be a career woman."

"Tell her it's a lot like being a career man."

"Yes, well, it would be easier if you told her. I mean, I haven't hit the problems head on."

"Sure. I'll try. Tell her to come in during office hours."

"Thanks, Jane."

She went into her office, wondering how many extra hours she had to put in counseling because she was one of only three women in the department. Many bright women were in graduate school now, the Betty Friedan generation. But those in her own generation had started grad work in the late fifties, and were now struggling to give the younger ones a hand up just when important things like tenure were emerging in their own careers. Maybe Linc's student was right: maybe it was harder to be a woman in this damn business.

She picked up her briefcase, packed with papers from bright-eyed students in her undergraduate course, and headed home. There was another worry, she thought as she switched off the ignition outside the apartment building. The Volks needed attention; nasty rattle it was developing. The dealer, unfortunately, was inconveniently located in a small town halfway to Syracuse. Well, maybe it would consent to run a little longer.

Roger, his sock feet propped on the hassock, was reading the paper when she came in. "Hi, hon," he said, barely glancing up. He was so damn domestic, she might as well be married to him. "How was your day?"

"The usual," she said, hanging up her coat. "Do we have a drink in this dump?"

"Gin, vodka," he said. "Fix one for me too, okay?"

"Sure, hon," she said. He glanced up at the bite in her voice but wisely decided not to comment on it. She went to the kitchen and found vodka and orange juice. She fixed two drinks and brought them back to the living room.

"Want some paper?" He handed her the front pages as he took

his drink. He waved the glass at her in a sort of vestigial toast and drank.

She kicked off her own shoes and curled into a chair to inspect the front page. "Hey, incredible! McCarthy got forty-two percent!"

"Yeah, isn't that amazing?"

"This war may finish Johnson yet." She flipped down to the bottom half of the page. "Oh God, that rapist is out murdering people again."

"Yeah. Watch it if you drive to Syracuse."

"God, what an awful way to die! Beaten and terrified, and then knifed. I'd prefer something quick."

"Such as?" he inquired.

Jane had thought about the question, on bad days. But now she answered casually, "Struck by lightning. Or at least a necrophiliac. Knifed before, not after."

"No. I'd prefer modern technology. The electric chair."

"Yeah, except you'd be locked up first. That's not for me."

"Well, most deaths are unpleasant," he said cheerfully, turning to the funnies.

"Wonder how he gets them off the road?" Jane said. "We were trying to figure it out today. They all seem to stop on highway ramps. Why?"

"I wouldn't know." He was not much interested; he was reading the comics.

"Speaking of roads," said Jane, "the Volks has to go to Schellsburg soon."

"Hell!"

"Yeah, this is the last time I buy an out-of-town car."

"An out-of-town lemon."

"The last one was pretty good, actually. But this one's been a mess."

"Well, how about Thursday? We can take it out early. I'll be in the office all day. You can keep mine."

"Fine. I'll need it. I have to talk to a martial arts expert at lunchtime. WAR wants some instruction."

"That's taking a lot of your time."

"I know. But these kids are mad, Roger. So am I."

"Yeah. It's not fair."

"About the Volks. Linc lives out in that direction. He'll probably give me a ride out to pick it up, so you won't have to."

34

"Okay. We'll do that."

Neither one of them felt like preparing dinner, so they picked up some Kentucky Fried Chicken and a bottle of Chablis. "If you can't have elegance, fake it," declared Roger, lighting the candles. He cleared up afterward and loaded the dishwasher. Jane, putting away the unfinished wine bottle, studied him surreptitiously. An agreeable man, dark-haired, a sexy smile. Conservatively dressed, of course. Lawyers always were. Horn-rimmed glasses. Mild-mannered Clark Kent. A junior member of a Laconia law firm, he was very fond of the town. One of the many advantages of tenure would be not having to move away from Roger.

"Well, what's the verdict?" he asked, catching her eyes on him.

"I didn't know I was being so obvious."

"I've got that legal-eagle eye."

"X-ray vision. Superman."

"No, not quite."

"I mean, that was the verdict. Mild-mannered Clark Kent, actually."

"That's more like it."

"Do you think of me as Lois Lane?"

"Hardly. You never require rescuing."

"Superwoman?" She flexed her arm.

He flicked on the dishwasher switch and turned to her seriously. "I think of you as you," he said. "My bright and tough and tender lover."

He could do that to her, shift unexpectedly to a level of warmth and intimacy that dissolved her worries and woke her hunger for him. "That's how I think of you too," she confessed. They moved into each other's arms.

She had to get up later to read the undergraduate papers, and it was nearly two before she finally got to sleep. Roger, bless him, did not noticeably contribute to efficiency.

IV

13 Tzikin
(March 21, 1968)

"I'm sorry, Mary Beth. This just wouldn't be enough."

"But I was hoping so much that I could finish by the end of summer, Professor Greene."

"No one can write a thesis that fast, Mary Beth. It'll take you most of this term to transcribe your tapes and organize the data. Then the real work starts."

Professor Greene was in her fifties, a vigorous gray-haired woman with wise eyes sunk in dark pouches that gave her the look of a sagacious raccoon. She had made her mark in the World War II years describing American Indian languages.

Mary Beth tried again. "But wouldn't a straightforward description of the language be just as valuable?"

The professor smiled. "Maybe, Mary Beth. For Bible translators and such, even more valuable. But if you want to be a linguist today, you have to go beyond your data to a theoretical discussion."

"I see." Damn. Professor Greene was right, of course.

"It would be no favor to you to grant a degree for a purely descriptive report. It would be wasted effort. You'd have no publications grow out of it, no talks. But if you do it right, you'll be launched toward a reputation in the field. You have the potential." Professor Greene frowned at Mary Beth's downcast face. "What's the problem, Mary Beth? You've been so depressed ever since you got back. Are you ill?"

"No, I just want to finish. To go away. To go back."

"It's easy to get attached to our field work."

"But not wise, you mean," Mary Beth added after a moment.

"I can't make personal decisions for you. I can only advise. But yes, that's my opinion, from an academic and career point of view."

"I suppose you're right." Mary Beth's voice was so small she could hardly hear it herself. She picked up the modified thesis proposal that Professor Greene had just rejected and tried to sound normal. "Well, I'll go back to the original proposal, then."

"It'll be better in the long run, Mary Beth. It was a good proposal. Theoretically interesting."

"If I do finish it early, will you accept it early?"

"Of course. But I don't want you to get your hopes up in vain. Finishing by the end of next year will be speedy work indeed. The end of this summer would be nearly impossible."

"Okay. Thank you, Professor Greene."

Mary Beth made her despondent way home. Maggie was just arriving too. With a guest.

"Hi, Mary Beth. Meet Frank Pinelli."

He was well built and casually dressed. A swatch of dark hair kept creeping toward his eyes and had to be tossed back frequently. "Hi," he said shyly.

"Hi. Are you in math too, Frank?"

"No. French lit. I'm just in Laconia for the afternoon. To see my adviser."

"And to shoot a few baskets," Maggie added. "I was down at the Y teaching my girls' gymnastics class, and couldn't help noticing that every time he missed he said *'Merde!'*"

He smiled. "And then I sank one, and couldn't help noticing that someone burst into the *Marseillaise.*"

Mary Beth smiled too. "I see."

"He just came over to borrow a book," said Maggie. "I'll go get it, Frank." But Mary Beth, watching him watch Maggie as she ran upstairs, was alarmed. He had more on his mind than a book.

They sat on the sofa for a few minutes, turning the pages and reading to each other in French. Mary Beth, on dinner duty that day, could hear them in the background as, depressed but determined, she cut up potatoes. She was able to use the little paring knives with no trouble. Not the long ones yet.

After a few moments she heard Jackie come in the front door.

"Hey, Jackie, do you know Frank?" asked Maggie.

37

"No, I guess not."

"Frank Pinelli, Jackie Edwards. You're both grads in French. Why don't you know each other?"

"Big department," explained Frank. "And I'm working in Syracuse while I finish my thesis, teaching a few classes at a prep school. I don't get over here to Laconia often."

"Well, glad to meet you," said Jackie. "What brings you here today?"

"Mostly reminding my adviser I'm alive. But I also learned that Maggie here owns a book I need for my thesis, so I'm buttering her up."

They talked a few minutes, then Jackie went upstairs. Soon Frank and Maggie appeared at the kitchen door.

"Mary Beth, Frank and I thought we'd go out for a quick dinner somewhere."

"There's plenty here," said Mary Beth, who had put in a couple of extra potatoes. "Can you stay?"

"Well, is it really no problem?" he asked, pushing back his wayward hair.

"None at all. Glad to have you." But she wished he wouldn't look at Maggie that way.

After dinner he left promptly, promising to return Maggie's book next week. Jackie turned to Maggie and said, "Nice guy."

"Yeah, I thought so."

"I like his eyes. But listen, Maggie, before I meet Peter tonight, I have a favor to ask. I need a statistician."

"My God, Jackie!" exclaimed Sue. "Are you deserting the true religion for hers?"

"Hush, Sue. It's about a project that a friend of mine from high school did. Sonia Michaelson. She did some work for her senior honors in education at Graham College a few years ago, on how little kids learn negatives. Reaction-time method. She tested dozens of kids. It was hours and hours of work. Everybody was very impressed, but it didn't come out statistically. They gave her honors anyway, but Sonia was disillusioned and changed fields. She's in international community planning now, and when I saw her over vacation she was getting ready to leave for Egypt. But she loaned me a copy of her original data. Maggie, could you look at it and tell me if it really *is* statistically worthless?"

"I can tell you about the numbers. Probably not the scientific value. I'm no linguist."

"I'll vouch for the science. Sonia's good," said Jackie. "If it's not hopeless, then I want to do something similar with French kids. They have those *ne pas* and *ne plus* negatives to learn."

"Will you have to test dozens of kids too?" asked Mary Beth.

"No, this would just be a class project for Freeman's seminar, maybe four or five kids. I don't want to waste my time on it if Sonia's paper is garbage. But it might be interesting."

"Sure. Let's look at it," said Maggie.

They sat at the dining room table to pore over the data sheets. An hour later Mary Beth, on her way to the kitchen to make coffee, saw that the calculator was out. "Checking her arithmetic?"

"No," said Jackie importantly. "We're taking the reciprocals of their reaction times."

"You're what?"

Maggie smiled at Mary Beth's expression. "It's a common first step in analyzing reaction-time experiments. If a kid stops to scratch or sneeze before he answers, you'll get a slow reaction time even if the question was easy. This technique gives you better data if you have some suspiciously slow responses."

"So you can fix the problem with math? That's clever!"

"You see why the Maya made us priests."

A few minutes later, with a delighted smile, Jackie announced that the new analysis had worked. "Wow!" she said, standing up to go meet Peter. "I've got to write Sonia! Except I can't. I don't know where she is in Egypt. Well, she'll be back home in August."

"Funny her advisers didn't suggest this," said Maggie. "It's a standard technique."

"Well, she said the guy in charge of the honors program was in counseling, and probably didn't do reaction-time things. They had to get an outside reader from the psych department for her at the last minute."

"Still, it's such an obvious thing to do." Maggie frowned at the rows of numbers, then stood up and followed Mary Beth to the kitchen. "Hey, was that boiling water I heard out here?"

"Yes. I made some coffee."

"Enough for me too?"

"It's Ixil style." Mary Beth smiled. "Better taste it first."

At the first sip the blue eyes widened. "Good Lord," said Maggie. Mary Beth laughed. Frowning, Maggie took another swallow. "What in the world is in this?"

"Chili."

"Good Lord," said Maggie again. She took another sip. "It grows on you, doesn't it? But it's not coffee."

"I like it. It reminds me of being there."

Maggie hoisted herself smoothly to perch on the kitchen table. "You know, you haven't told me much about Guatemala. What's it like there? Hot?"

"No. The Ixil live high in the mountains, and there's lots of rain and fog. Cold sometimes. You can see your breath."

"I can see why they dose their coffee with chili."

"Yes, that helps. And they have warm clothes. But it can be very pleasant. The mountains are beautiful, Maggie. The Cuchumatanes, they're called. On market days all the people come in from the different villages, the women dressed in their own village designs. Red ones from Nebaj and Chajul, blue and green from San Juan Cotzal. The little babies are so cute, all wrapped up with little caps on, and tied onto their mothers' backs."

Maggie smiled. She was drinking the coffee; maybe she did like it.

"There are earthquakes—and volcanoes aren't far away," Mary Beth continued. "That's a little frightening. Living on this little thin crust over molten rock that might erupt at any minute. The whole country is like that. It's like borrowed time."

"Well, we have floods and tornadoes here."

"Somehow it's different. I mean, think of it, Maggie, the earth quaking, erupting. Water is supposed to move, and air. Floods and tornadoes are bad, but they're just quantitative changes. But the earth is unmoving, solid, the reference point for the motion of other things. When you can't depend on that basic fact, everything else seems unpredictable and arbitrary."

"It must make you feel helpless."

"No, that's not why," murmured Mary Beth, then came back to herself and looked up, startled. "I mean, it does, but you also feel that everything is alive. Gods everywhere. In the wind and the corn. In the mountains. In the rain. In the earth."

"So the Maya were right."

"Yes. But of course today the real threat is human. The death squads, the civil war, the poverty, the malnutrition."

"It must be depressing to work there."

"Yes. But it would be even worse not to. They are splendid people, Maggie. We should record the culture, help if we can. I'm

40

only doing a little bit, of course, but everything we learn is helpful. Mostly to us.''

"To us?''

"Because we need to learn about human unity and diversity. We know so little.''

"You think we can learn? Look at black history. Or the draft calls. Three hundred thousand gook killers at a time for Vietnam. Maybe your Maya have got off easy.''

"Maybe,'' said Mary Beth dubiously.

"You mean bombs are at least quicker than poverty and malnutrition?''

"Oh, I know the bombs leave the survivors poor and hungry too. But it's so sad. One of the people I worked with—Ros—tried to give me her baby. Said I could provide for him better.''

"Poor woman!'' Maggie was shaken.

After a glum moment Mary Beth said, "Hey, listen, it would probably be more cheerful to talk about you.''

"I thought Sue's quiz had pretty well covered my background.''

"Well, I know you're musical, and you've lived in France.'' Mary Beth had helped her new housemate unload her old, rusty, perfectly tuned blue Ford. Maggie's room now contained a wide-ranging record collection, a French rabbit coat, a Comédie Française poster, and bookends that looked like Notre Dame; math books and flute music filled the bookshelves, while another box of books—Shaw, Molière, and Shakespeare—had been shoved into a closet. "But,'' added Mary Beth, "Sue didn't even ask you where you're from.''

"Ohio, near Cincinnati. Dad's a professor, Mom's the mayor.''

"The mayor! Wow.'' Mary Beth paused, then added daringly, "And you sidestepped Sue's question about men.''

The dark blue eyes were opaque. "Yeah, okay, let's just say I'm getting over the cliché unhappy love affair.''

Mary Beth considered. "Not cliché.''

Maggie smiled a little. "Thank you. Yeah. He was remarkable.''

"You seem okay now. Frank was impressed.''

"Oh, I'm functioning again. I went home and cried on my mom's shoulder, and then got myself busy.''

"Twenty-one hours of math.''

"Right. And now I'm in control of my life again, and I plan to stay that way. I don't want to look back.''

That meant it still hurt, Frank or no Frank. "Yeah," Mary Beth said, "I don't either. I mean, I understand that."

"Are you sure?" Maggie asked gently. "Sure you don't want to talk?"

"Me? Nothing to talk about." She didn't sound convincing even to herself.

After a moment Maggie said, "Okay, I understand. Maybe later." She hopped off the table and started washing out her mug.

For an instant Mary Beth wondered if she should tell, but the thought brought such panic that she couldn't face it. Forget—she must just push it away and forget.

Frank returned on Wednesday afternoon, Maggie's book in one hand and a Syracuse newspaper in the other.

"How about a flick tonight?" he asked Maggie. "There's a good one in Syracuse. Truffaut's *400 Blows.*"

"Great! I'll take my own car, okay?"

"You sure? I don't mind driving. I like it."

"So do I. I'll just meet you there."

"You're a free spirit." He had a shy, slow smile, an exploratory beginning that widened into a warm grin.

Mary Beth, waking from a dream of knives at three o'clock in the morning, went to the window and looked out at the dead March world, deeply gray but cut by jagged bars of light from the street lamps. The sun was on its way through the underworld now, the Maya would say, but it still had many trials to endure before its rebirth. Hun-Came and Vucub-Came ruled now. An oppressive time of night. Maggie's car, she noticed, was not in its usual place in the driveway. She shouldn't worry. Long ago she herself had spent nights with Tip. Long, long ago. She tried to remember those nights, Tip's little jokes, his hands warm and welcome on her skin, but it was gone. Another time, another world, forever gone.

Eventually she managed to sleep again, and at seven-thirty woke to find Maggie waiting for her, bright-eyed and ready for their usual morning run. Her car was in the driveway now. As they ran out side by side into the tentative early light, Mary Beth asked, "Did you have fun last night?"

"Yes. Interesting film. We went to his place afterward and had fondue."

"Well, if he feeds you he can't be all bad."

42

Maggie, used to being teased about her robust appetite, smiled and put on a burst of speed that saved her from further comment.

The rattle and boom of heavy drums and the electric whine of a guitar split the air. Mary Beth, just sitting down at her desk after dinner that night, jumped up. She ran back into the hall to find the others there too. Sue had clapped her hands despairingly over her ears, and Jackie was the one who spoke.

"Damn! Our ugly secret is out, Sue."

"Who is it?" asked Mary Beth over the pounding music.

"Across the street. Five undergraduate business majors trying to be their own mini-frat," said Sue. "They moved in right after you left. They don't feel manly unless the volume is set at banshee level."

"They're probably deaf," said Jackie kindly. "Actually it's not bad when their doors are closed. But it's warm tonight."

"Okay," said Sue, "who's going to tell them to turn it down?"

"I'll go." Maggie headed resolutely down the stairs.

"Wait, I'll come too," said Mary Beth. The two of them crossed the street to the square frame house that faced them, trembling with amplified sound. Maggie gave a perfunctory knock on the open front door and sailed on in. A stocky young man starting up the stairs looked around in surprise.

"Just a minute," he shouted. Maggie and Mary Beth followed him to the big stereo, the major piece of furniture in the living room. Maggie watched closely as he turned down the volume.

"Hi," she said. "We're from across the street."

"Oh God, could you hear it over there? I didn't know it was up that loud. I'm Bill."

"Maggie." She was peering admiringly at the back of the amplifier. "These big outfits sneak up on you," she said sympathetically. "A lot of power."

A second young man with slick, dark hair had appeared in the doorway. The first glanced back at him and said, "This is Todd. Todd, this is Maggie from across the street."

"And this is Mary Beth. Hi, Todd." Maggie gave him a bright smile, which was not returned, and looked back at Bill. "Maybe you could keep the doors and windows closed, okay?"

"Okay," said Bill cheerfully. Todd still glowered.

"Thanks," said Mary Beth, feeling unwelcome. "See you around."

Maggie closed the door carefully behind them. They were half-way down the front steps when the volume rose again, a little, behind them. They exchanged a resigned glance.

As they came up their own front walk, a chipmunk darted across in front of them. From somewhere behind her breastbone, the wave of terror surged through Mary Beth. She stumbled on the steps and caught herself on the rough brick of the porch column.

"You okay?" asked Maggie, concerned.

"Yeah. It startled me." She kept her face hidden against the brick and tried to stop shaking.

"Yeah, he moved fast." Maggie waited patiently.

"Well." Mary Beth made an effort and straightened, pretended she wasn't nauseated. Would she ever be in control again? She forced her voice into a semblance of steadiness. "Let's get back to work."

"Okay." Maggie took her elbow and guided her back in to the refuge of her room and the thesis tapes.

Frank called Maggie twice the next week. The second time she replaced the receiver with a sad and reflective look.

"Bad news?" asked Jackie, who had answered it first.

"Yes. Old Maggie has blown it again. Another experiment bites the dust. Another living sacrifice at the shrine of my blunders." With which extravagant declaration she slammed into her room. Mary Beth and Jackie exchanged a startled glance.

On Friday afternoon, he came again. It was raining, and his dark hair was dripping a little into his collar.

"Maggie here?"

"Upstairs." Mary Beth went to get her. As they came back down, she noted the glow in his face in the instant before he masked it.

"Hi, Frank." Maggie was breezy. "Good to see you. What brings you here?"

"I thought maybe you'd like to see the Resnais tonight." He pushed back his damp hair.

She sounded regretful. "I've really got too much work this weekend, Frank. Maybe some other time."

"Oh." He tried to smile but couldn't get past the first tentative flicker. "I mean, well, I thought you wanted to."

"I did. But it turns out I can't."

"No way I could change your mind?"

44

"No, I'm afraid not."

"Next week?"

"No, it looks just like this weekend. Too busy."

Her voice was friendly but firm. He was genuinely upset, surprise and hurt and anger just under the surface. Clearly he had expected something else. "Well—all right. Guess I go back and see it by myself." He shoved his hands into the pockets of his rain jacket.

"May I go?" Jackie's gentle voice startled them all.

"You? Sure. I mean, I should have thought . . ." He was confused. "Sure, Jackie, that'd be great."

"Okay. Let me get my coat." She went to the hall closet. Frank was still looking at Maggie, suspicious now, and bitter.

"Not my idea," she said.

"You must have known I'd be here!"

"Frank, let's keep things straightforward, okay? I just can't go."

"But why?" He could no longer hide his anguish. Maggie, tense, still faced him squarely, eyes cold as sleet.

"Okay, Frank," she said. "If you want it public, here goes: I need my freedom. And we were beginning to find each other too damn attractive."

A brittle second passed. Then Jackie said, "Whoops. Maybe you don't want company." She had paused in belting her raincoat.

"On the contrary," he said unsteadily, "I really need it now."

"I won't go if you don't want me along," she said. "But I really did want to see the film."

"Okay," he said, voice rough. "But just promise me you won't be straightforward, like some people."

"Let's just go see the flick," she said soothingly. They went out into the rain.

For a few minutes Maggie prowled around the kitchen unhappily, then flung herself out into the rainy backyard, where she split firewood viciously until she dropped a log on her shoe. She came back in, limping and coated with mud. Mary Beth waited in the upstairs hall as she hobbled up.

"The Creature from the Black Lagoon," she said. "Can I help?"

"Nope," Maggie replied. "I'm just going to take a shower."

"Good idea."

"A cold one."

45

"Oh. But you were right to level with him, Maggie."

Acid blue eyes met hers. "Why don't you just shut up and enjoy your immunity?"

Mary Beth retreated into her room, stung. Maggie's arrows were rare, but swift and accurate.

Jackie was back by midnight, enthusiastic about the film.

V

6 Imush
(March 28, 1968)

This bitch was cagey. Most were stupid—opened their windows or even got out to talk to him. This one rolled the window down only a few inches, and even though he was very polite, she wouldn't open any further. "Never mind," he said at last, "I can see you're in a hurry. I'll manage." Suspicious bitch. He watched her drive away. Well, he'd be cagey too. No stories tomorrow in the newspaper for her to think about, tell the police about. The police were stupid; the bitches controlled them too, them and their sweaty blue shirts.

He waited to be sure she was out of sight, then drove across the intersection, up the ramp, onto the highway. He'd take the little beagle to a vet. He smiled to himself. Even if this bitch accused him, he was safe. Syracuse was huge. And he was on his way up, respectable, intelligent. Respectable occupation, respectable home. They'd never believe he was the one. They'd think it was some bum. One of the advantages of his work was that he wasn't stuck in an office, didn't have to punch a clock.

Mum's puppy hadn't been a beagle. A solid tan dog, curly ears. Maybe a golden retriever. Pa saying, "You think I won't?" The knife against the curly tan throat. Mum shrieking, dropping the shotgun. Pa saying, "Shut up, you're scaring the boy." He was scared now. No. No, not now. Not scared. Angry, that was it! Because this suspicious bitch had forced him to wait. She hadn't been like Mum, like the others. Was she controlling him? No, of course not, he was controlling her. Vet first. Then back to work. Quick. Respectable.

"La wat-ʔin," said Ros's gentle voice from the machine.

Mary Beth loved to transcribe her tapes. Slipping into her beloved Mayan was like escaping her present useless self. It was important to record the language and culture of the brave warm people she had known, who clung to their proud past with a justified tenacity understood by too few. And for Mary Beth, the voices on the tapes awakened the mountain scents, the bright colors, the friendly smiles of Ros and other friends, the optimism and confidence of her own younger, stronger self. When she dared think about it, she was surprised. The television news now, with its accounts of battle and death in Vietnam, confirmed her pessimism; it was a bad world. But Guatemala too had been filled with cause for pessimism, with violence always lurking behind the beautiful surface, with poverty and illness common, with injustice a constant fact of life. Why did Ixil give her such strength? But it did. From the flat tasteless world of her depression she was able, for a few hours each day, to slip into the brighter world of her work.

Running helped sometimes. And music. Maggie had found a chunky red-haired mathematician named Dan Reade who played clarinet well, and their quintet met for practice now once or twice a week.

And once when Jackie and Peter talked her into accompanying them to the university theatre production of *The Crucible,* Mary Beth discovered afterward with a sense of shock that she had not had a bad thought in three whole hours. She had always enjoyed theatre, but now it seemed to have the power to absorb her completely. She resolved to go whenever she could.

But the most consistent solace was her work. She wrote now, *"La wat-ʔin,* 'I will sleep,' "* and pushed the start button again for "I am sleeping."

"N un-wat-ʔe," said Ros.

Uh-oh, thought Mary Beth, recording the words carefully. That doesn't fit. She switched on the tape again for "I slept." In the background she could hear Ros's toddler chattering.

"Kat wat-ʔin," said Ros's voice.

That was okay. *"Wat-ʔin"* was okay.

She made a list. To be a linguist, Professor Greene said, you had to have the soul of a clerk. And lots of three-by-five cards. Mary

Beth shuffled through her stack. Right, there it was, a transitive verb's pronoun. Why had Ros used it with the intransitive "am sleeping"?

Damn. Could Professor Greene be right? Maybe it would take longer—a year and a half without being able to escape back to Guatemala. I've got to do it sooner, she told herself fiercely. I'll figure it out. I've got to.

Cathy Berryman filled her sherry glass and asked, "Jane, quick, tell me what Corbett's lecture was about. Linc is always telling me I sound like a dummy, but I can't take that many hours away from Donny to come hear the lectures. So fill me in, okay?"

"Sure. Corbett is studying altruism," explained Jane. She and Cathy moved away from the bar that Dick Davies had set up in his dining room. "He was trying to show that people who feel they are to blame for something will behave more generously than people who are just innocent bystanders."

"Because they feel guilty?"

"That's what he thought. But, in fact, the Innocent Bystanders in his study were just as altruistic as the Guilties."

"I wonder why?"

"That's what they're arguing about right now."

Petra Davies, round and smiling in her baby blue dress, joined them. "Hello, Jane. You look lovely tonight!"

"Thank you." Jane was wearing her silk paisley, the one that Roger said made her eyes look green.

"So glad you could come, Cathy," Petra went on. "How's Donny doing?"

"Fine! The nursery school says he's just like his dad," said Cathy proudly. "Loves animals. They've got rabbits and gerbils and parakeets, and Donny gives all the other kids instructions about taking care of them."

"Doesn't he have pets at home?" asked Petra.

"Of course! Five cats, a German shepherd, and two snakes."

"Oh dear."

"Donny adores them. He's writing a book, he says, about the snakes. Of course it's only three pages long so far."

"Excuse me." Jane left Cathy and Petra to discuss the Berryman child. Her interest in little Donny Berryman was strictly academic. Linc had brought Donny to campus for her to test a couple of years ago when she was beginning her work with prelinguistic

49

babies. But now he was four, an accomplished speaker of his native tongue, and beyond the murky beginnings that fascinated Jane professionally.

There was another danger, she had found. As a female psychologist who studied infants and children, it was all too easy to be viewed as a sort of super nursery school teacher. During her first year she had occasionally tried to discuss linguistic development with mothers, but usually her comments were interpreted as signs of interest in the particular child and she soon found herself embroiled in a discussion of formulas or toilet training. She, who had never changed a diaper in her life. Maybe someday, if she got tenure, she and Roger would raise a family. But not soon. Her children now were the articles and the slowly forming book, and they needed all her attention. She joined the small mob of faculty and graduates around the guest of honor, Professor Corbett.

"But why?" Dick Davies was asking. "It's all very well to say the Guilties were generous because they wanted to make up for their supposed sin. But it doesn't explain the Innocent Bystanders. You need a motive that will explain both groups."

"We couldn't think of one," admitted Corbett.

"Why do the two groups have to have the same motive?" Maggie Ryan asked. "Suppose the Innocent Bystanders have a sort of general belief in justice, in good outweighing evil. Every one of us is responsible for making it a just world."

Corbett was interested. "So the source of their altruism is some sort of felt obligation to adjust the scales? If something goes wrong, you counter with your own good deed? But that's pretty abstract if you aren't actually guilty."

"Very abstract," agreed Jane. "An attempt for a just world."

"Maybe the Guilties felt that way too," suggested Dick. "Maybe it's one motive after all."

"Maybe," said Jane, "but it could be different. Guilt is part of eye-for-an-eye justice. The misdeed and the punishment in perfect proportion. Individualized, ideal justice. But the abstract principles Maggie is talking about are what motivate people in civil rights groups or peace groups or the Peace Corps. Caring for people. Not just personal atonement."

"I see," said Corbett. "I never killed Vietnamese villagers personally, but it's still up to me to help stop the war?"

"Right," said Jane. "Although you'd also feel obliged to fix things you personally had damaged."

"Yes, I'll work on that," said Corbett.

"Anyone else for a refill?" asked Dick, waving his empty glass.

"I'll go with you," said Jane.

As they walked toward the bar she heard Maggie ask Corbett, "I know you're interested in altruism. Donations to charity and so forth. But the motives you're studying could lead to other types of behavior too. What about revenge, someone who forces some other guilty person to correct the scales, whether he wants to or not? Or what about people who feel individually guilty, but hurt themselves, instead of helping others?"

Interesting questions, thought Jane. Human behavior was much more complicated than Corbett's little model allowed. Than anyone's model allowed. But she abandoned the train of thought because Dick was pouring her sherry and asking, "Enough?"

"Yes, thanks."

"Roger isn't here tonight."

"No, he sends his apologies. He's busy on a tough case."

"Tell me, Jane. Do you plan to marry soon?"

"Why do you ask?"

"Just curiosity."

"Yes, I can see that it would be an interesting question. I wonder if Hal will marry soon? Or, on the other hand, if Linc and Cathy plan to divorce soon?"

"Yes, interesting questions all." Dick took a sip of sherry, his blue eyes twinkling in cheerful defeat. "I agree that family has nothing to do with our work, Jane. I mean, God, my own father was arrested for assault once, so I'd be the last to complain about your private background. It's just that in the past we've had a couple of excellent women professors resign in order to marry."

"This one won't."

"Yes, of course, I wasn't implying that."

The hell you weren't, thought Jane. She said, "All the same, Dick, let me repeat that I am totally committed to my research and teaching. I love it."

"Yes, of course. Do you have any preference? Between research and teaching?"

"Oh, you know how much variety there is in both. Rewards and frustrations. It's exhilarating when you do an experiment that gives you a glimpse into the way people work. It's also wonderful to get a good paper from a student. I enjoy both sides."

"Of course, experiments don't always work out."

"And students sometimes disappoint you. Just today, I had to fail a young man because he'd altered data on a midterm project. Wanted it to be statistically significant, so he changed the numbers."

"You failed him?"

"Had to. It was premeditated cheating. I can bear with ignorance or laziness, Dick. But altering data strikes at the heart of what science is trying to do. It's an attack on truth."

"Well, failing him may be a bit extreme. But you're right to nip it in the bud. By the way, I just read your articles on mothers' speech to young children. Quite good."

"Thanks." Jane was proud of that series of three articles, based on her long-ago thesis. "I have a student working in Canada on the same variables with French speakers."

"You language people are lucky. Your area of investigation is so clearly marked off, and the next steps are so obvious. It's easy to tell whether something is or isn't language. In social psych we have problems. Where does motivation stop? What are the edges of personality?"

Jane smiled. "We scientists are hopeless romantics, aren't we? We all have these secret images of ourselves smashing through jungles of ignorance, like Balboa or Davy Crockett."

"Our armor a lab coat, our weapon a rapierlike intelligence." Dick was amused by her metaphor.

Linc Berryman, big and dark-bearded and jovial, joined them. "Hello, hello!"

"Hi, Linc."

"Jane, I was just talking to Terry Poole. Tell me, what's this I hear about WAR?"

"War?" asked Dick.

"Our militant acronym for Women Against Rape," explained Jane. "I'm a sort of figurehead faculty adviser for a group of women who want to reduce the incidence of rape. Especially against themselves."

"Any special reason they chose you?"

"I was handy, female, and altruistic," said Jane. "I suppose Corbett would put me in the Innocent Bystanders group. We were all upset by the Christie James murder."

"I see. What does the group do?"

"We've only had two meetings so far. We plan to study all aspects of the situation—from prevention to self-defense to the psychology of rapists.''

"And just what is the psychology of the rapist?"

"I'm not in psychopathology," Jane said, smiling. "But I gather there are many varieties. Rapists who first gain a woman's confidence, may even date her, come from all classes. But a man who rapes strangers is often young, from a low socioeconomic class, abused as a child, violence-prone, and angry at women for some reason, maybe unsure of his own sexuality. Most don't care who the victim is as long as she's female.''

"I was surprised that this fellow who killed Christie James also killed that old woman on the thirteenth," said Dick.

"Yes. Most of us think of rape as a crime of passion, some poor fellow overcome by desire for some seductive woman. But it's not true. They're angry, not horny. That's the frightening thing. All those pointers Mother gave us about wearing high necklines and not smiling at strangers have nothing to do with it. Any female will do as a victim.''

"God, this is an unpleasant discussion," said Dick.

But Linc persevered. "You make it sound like a mugging."

"It is like a mugging. The same guys sometimes do both. But being able to describe a typical rapist doesn't help the victim much.''

"What does?" asked Linc.

"We're looking into that next. Check back later," she temporized, glancing at Dick. He was staring at his sherry as though it contained a worm, and she hoped Linc would not go on.

"Nowadays it's hard to feel safe even in your own home," said Dick. After a pause he looked up at Jane and Linc. "Can I freshen your drinks?"

"No, thanks," said Jane. "In fact, I'd better be off. I promised my psycholinguistics class I'd get their papers back tomorrow.''

She'd left her briefcase and raincoat in the bedroom. As she shrugged into her coat, the case fell and snapped open. Damn, all that junk. She dropped to her knees. Pens, coin purse, keys, letter-knife, appointment book. Anything else? Valium. Where was it? She didn't see the little bottle. She felt next to the nightstand, under the bed. Something round. But not the bottle, she realized suddenly. The handle of a knife, a long knife. She pushed it back hastily and lifted the edge of the bedspread. God, there were four of them, four knives. Hard to feel safe even in your own home, he'd said. She pitied the burglar who tried the Davies bedroom.

The Valium, she saw, had lodged between two knives. She scooped it into the briefcase and hurried out.

The Volks coughed a time or two in protest before starting. Still not quite fixed. She eased it into gear and proceeded cautiously into the traffic lane, depressed to think of taking it yet again to the dealer.

The night was not quite clear, a faint cold haze visible around the streetlights. No doubt it was her imagination, or the knives, or the talk about rapists. But it seemed to her that a light-colored car that pulled onto the road behind her a block from Dick's was following her. She locked both doors when she stopped for a traffic light, and parked at the well-lit front of her apartment building instead of going into the dark garage. Roger was home; she could see the light of their living room through the drapes. She waited until the pale car went past, then hurried up the stairs and into the apartment.

"Anything wrong, honey?" asked Roger.

"No. Too much of Dick's sherry, I guess," said Jane. She kissed his dark head, and felt safe, and kicked herself for being so old-fashioned.

VI

7 Iiq—12 Chee
(March 29—April 3, 1968)

"Maria Markaao was the daughter of a god," explained Mary Beth. "Her admirer Oyew Achi was a god too, but her father didn't like him. So Oyew Achi thought of a plan. He turned himself into a hummingbird. Maria saw the bird and was delighted with it. She was a fine weaver, like most Ixil women, and she told people that she needed the bird to use as a pattern. They caught it for her and brought it to her room. Once the door was closed, he turned back into a man."

"Shouting, 'Surprise!' " said Maggie.

"No doubt. Well, Maria apparently found him as attractive as the bird. They locked the door, and the father found out the next morning that he now had a married daughter."

"Ah, sweet young love. And this is the bird in question?" Maggie, doing splits on the hearthrug, inspected the design woven into the blanket that covered the old sofa.

"So Ros tells me."

"And Maria and her husband lived happily ever after?"

"Well, no. Her dad had to accept the marriage, but he continued to hassle them in various ways. They overcame most of his tricks, but eventually he succeeded in hitting Maria with a lightning bolt. Today her spirit is splintered into a variety of animals."

"A sad end." Maggie was now practicing a backbend and spoke upside down. "I like the Ixil stories. A lot more realistic than happily-ever-after."

"They aren't very romantic people. If anyone ever had reason to know that life is unfair and cruel, it's the Ixil."

"God, Maggie, are you stuck?" asked Jackie, looking in. Maggie was still in her backbend.

"No. Just doing stretches."

Jackie plopped herself onto the sofa next to Mary Beth and eyed Maggie solemnly. "I asked Frank to come to dinner tonight."

Maggie righted herself abruptly. "Will you want me to leave?"

"No." Jackie sounded determined. "I like him a lot, Maggie."

"Sure."

"The first two times I saw him, you were all he talked about."

"Sounds boring."

Jackie grinned. "He's thought of other topics since. But you see, I want to know where I stand before I get too involved."

"Okay, kid. I'll help."

It was awkward at first. Frank, though civil, was stiff and ill-at-ease. Maggie, too, had somehow subdued her vitality, her wide sunshiny smile, almost to the point of dowdiness. But slowly, under the combination of her polite reserve and Jackie's warmth, he relaxed. Everyone became comfortable again from then on.

Except Peter.

The *Times* front page was jammed with immense headlines. President Johnson had announced that he would not run again. Eugene McCarthy and Robert Kennedy and Hubert Humphrey scrambled to better their chances for the Democratic nomination. Richard Nixon was securely ahead among the Republicans.

In Guatemala, Archbishop Casariego was kidnapped, then found alive in Chichicastenango, a bit south of Ixil country.

"Who's he?" asked Maggie. This evening she was lounging at the other end of the sofa, doodling on her calculator.

"Important in the church. Right before I left in December, he publicly asked the government to account for some people who had been arrested and disappeared while in police custody."

"An awkward request?"

"Yes. There were two hundred seventy-some people on his list," said Mary Beth.

"God! Do you think the government kidnapped him?"

"I'd guess right-wing terrorists plus the army. But the president is firing some of the top men. So the archbishop may be just an excuse for the president to get rid of a few top rivals."

"Will it make any difference to your Ixil?"

"I don't know. Sometimes I think they'd be better off just giving in, not fighting. What would you choose, Maggie? A life of safe drudgery and poverty and malnutrition? Or a faint chance to bring justice? No, not even that, there's really no chance for justice at all."

"A faint chance to screw the bastards keeping me down?"

"That's it."

"Well, that's what I'd choose."

"Even if it got your family in trouble?" She was remembering Ros, the fierce sacrificial protectiveness toward her children.

Maggie got up, restless, and went to look out the window at the rotting gray snow revealing patches of dead earth. "I'm afraid so," she said. "I've done it before, Mary Beth. I try not to, but I have this talent, it seems, for sacrificing other people."

"What do you mean?"

"My family and friends are doomed to flounder in the wake of my ill-conceived crusades."

"We're not talking alarm clocks. We're talking about civil war and death."

"Well, I have to admit I haven't encountered any civil wars yet," she said consideringly. Mary Beth noticed the omission, and was chilled. Maggie turned back, the fading light picking out the line of cheekbone and square jaw. "But if I ever do, Mary Beth, be warned. *Sauve qui peut.* Sink or swim."

"I'll remember. Do your friends complain?"

"Oh, yeah. They kick and scream. But so far, luckily, my friends have mostly turned out to be swimmers."

Sue was coming in from the library, arms loaded with books with Cyrillic titles. "What an odd requirement for friendship," she observed, dumping the books on the table. "I can dog-paddle. Will that count?"

"No, not good enough. But fortunately for you, we were merely extending a metaphor," said Maggie.

"A metaphor. Good. Literature may yet triumph over Pythagoras," said Sue approvingly. "Listen, Swede, speaking of literature, are we going to *The Three Sisters?*"

"Of course!" Mary Beth went to the theatre whenever she could talk someone into accompanying her. Since Frank had begun monopolizing Jackie's evenings and Maggie never went, it was more difficult. But Sue wanted to see the Chekhov.

"Well, they're already sold out for both Saturdays," reported Sue. "But we can get good seats on weekdays. Say this Wednesday."

"Let's try for Wednesday. Want to come, Maggie? Chekhov?"

"No, thanks."

"Why not?" She hadn't wanted to see *The Crucible* either, or the studio theatre Ionesco. But suddenly Mary Beth had an image of that box of books in the closet upstairs, Shakespeare and Molière and Shaw. And Chekhov.

"I just don't," said Maggie mildly, but there was a warning edge in the pleasant voice. Mary Beth ignored it.

"But how can you give up something as wonderful as theatre?"

There was a flash of anger in the blue eyes. "How can you give up chipmunks and white metal doors?"

The room dimmed suddenly as the underworld engulfed her. Mary Beth's damp forehead fell onto her palms. Hun-Came and Vucub-Came shrieked with laughter inside her head. Chipmunks and white metal doors! The chanting rang in her terrified ears. No, it wasn't chanting. It wasn't the Lords of Death. It was Sue, repeating it in bewilderment. "Chipmunks? White metal doors? What the hell are you two talking about?" And then Maggie's strong penitent arm around her shoulders.

"It's okay, Mary Beth. Everything's okay. I'm a klutz."

"Oh God, Maggie." The Lords of Death retreated reluctantly.

"Everything's okay. Really."

"Come on, kiddo," said Sue, worried. "Everything's cool. We didn't mean to say the magic words. Didn't even know them."

"I did," said Maggie. "I was mad as hell. But it won't happen again. I promise." Gentle bony fingers were stroking Mary Beth's long hair back from her face.

"Okay, look, it's nothing," she managed to say. But she felt exposed, as though the secret she had been laboring so carefully to conceal was open for all to read.

"Good," said Sue briskly. "That's the spirit." She gave Mary Beth a concerned glance, but continued, "Okay, Wednesday, two tickets, right?"

"Right," said Mary Beth, straightening a little. The panic had subsided into exhaustion. Maggie's supporting arm, like a protective wing, was still around her shoulders.

Maggie said, "Three tickets."

"Really?" asked Sue, pleased.

"Yes."

"Maggie, are you sure?" Mary Beth blundered in with a clumsy, urgent anxiety.

"I'm sure that anything that makes me hurt my friends has got to go." Their eyes locked in mutual pain.

"But what if you're not ready?"

"The hell with being ready. The important thing is being in control. Nobody's going to decide for me what I do or don't do."

"Except, of course, for yours truly, the collective conscience." Sue's husky voice broke in. "And, Maggie Ryan, I'm here to remind you that the guard has changed, and it's your night to take out the trash."

Maggie smiled at her. "Except, of course, for that," she said, and breezed off toward the kitchen. Mary Beth was left alone and apprehensive on the sofa.

Quintet practice that night was not a complete success. Sue and Maggie did all right, and from time to time Dan on the clarinet sounded almost inspired, his red hair tousled, his stubby fingers flickering on the keys. But Mary Beth still felt tired and dull, and Peter was worse. He greeted them with his usual wiry bounciness, but as it became clear to him that, once again, Jackie was not there to listen, he seemed to sag, and the oboe sections were dispirited and often inaccurate. They broke up a little early, and he packed up his instrument, refused the coffee they offered, and almost forgot to say good-bye as he left.

"So you're saying it's related to ongoing, incomplete actions?" asked Professor Greene.

"That's right. Like 'I am sleeping.' "

"That's very interesting, Mary Beth. Find something on the historical development, and you've got a paper right there."

"Yes. I'm looking at other Mayan languages now."

"Wonderful!" Professor Greene's pouched eyes creased in enthusiasm. "Keep it up, Mary Beth! Why don't you sketch out this section separately, and we'll submit it to the institute this summer?"

"Thank you. That's great, Professor Greene!" Mary Beth was pleased. That disturbing verb form that Ros had used had turned out to be a key to the whole system. The only problem was that it was clear it would take many months to work out the implications.

She stopped at Peter's on the way home. His roommate opened the door.

"Hi, Tom. Peter here?"

"No, he's got a late seminar today."

"Well, he borrowed my duckbill pliers last week to make some reeds. I need them back. Just found out my two extras are both split."

"You guys are crazy to have such temperamental instruments," said Tom. "They'll be in his room. Why don't you look around?"

"Thanks." Mary Beth went in. Peter's room was orderly, desk cleared, no dirty clothes. His reeds were almost done, she saw, and her pliers were laid neatly by the paraffin and wire on a bookshelf. Turning to leave, her attention was caught by the only chaotic place in the room, the wastebasket. Something familiar about that torn scrap. She leaned over, picked up a second scrap, and saw Jackie's photo, ripped into pieces.

"Did you find them?" called Tom.

"Yes. Thanks." Mary Beth tucked the pliers into her Guatemalan bag and left, the pleasure she had felt at Professor Greene's enthusiasm diminished by Peter's pain.

Monday night, when Jackie was away with Frank, the other three sat in the living room looking at the fuzzy cheap TV that Sue had inherited from her older brother. The late news came on. After a few scenes of wounded Vietnamese, burning villages, and stunned, bleeding children, Sue switched it off abruptly.

"Enough," she said. "I already knew the world was going to hell."

"No news there," agreed Mary Beth.

"I don't understand how anyone can think any purpose is worth all that." Sue's husky voice was troubled. "Do you think we'll ever get out?"

"Who knows?" said Maggie. "But Johnson's quitting, and look how well McCarthy's doing in the primaries."

"But we're still over there." Mary Beth gestured helplessly at the TV. "And ready to move into Guatemala and a dozen other places."

"The trouble with people for peace is that we don't have big guns and loud voices," declared Sue. "Everyone ignores us. We

60

should get up a crack military division. Don't you think they'd pay attention then? Whang between the eyes if they didn't.''

Mary Beth said feelingly, "God, I wish I was a man."

"How come? You don't like what they do. You don't even like them," said Sue, turning her resentment toward this new target. Maggie frowned at her but she went on defensively. "Well, look at us. Jackie's out fucking Frank, all red-blooded American woman-hood. But we three sit here, frustrated or not, I don't know, bad-mouthing men, blaming them for a war they're mostly against too, watching the years tick away."

There was a half-smile on Maggie's face. "Chanting faint hymns to the cold fruitless moon," she said. Mary Beth was re-minded again of the boxes of books that hadn't been unpacked.

"Right," Sue was saying. "So what is it? We all claim to be happy here. We haven't always been against males. In fact, Mary Beth had a hot thing going with Tip Warren last June before he went to Arizona and she skipped off south of the border. They were writing twice a week before she left. Right? Not a card since she got back and she doesn't even miss him. And despite the clouds of perfume she's started wearing, she says she'd rather be a man." She glowered at Mary Beth. "And I had some fun in my flaming youth too," she went on when Mary Beth said nothing. "But now I'm making like an embittered old maid. And judging from Frank, I think it's the same with you," she finished aggressively to Mag-gie.

"Sure," said Maggie softly. "I had a flaming youth too. I was very vulnerable. Not anymore. Never again." She was looking at Sue with understanding.

Sue seemed to have forgotten that Mary Beth was there. Her eyes were fixed on Maggie's. She said, almost tentatively, "Mine left and didn't even help with the abortion."

"Mine left too." Maggie reached out and took Sue's freckled hand. "But I didn't have an abortion. That's a hell of a thing to have to go through alone."

"God, yes," Sue remembered grimly. "It was in the back streets of Toledo, you know? Sooty brick. Filthy. And I had to go at night. It was so dirty. Now, I keep cleaning things all the time. Maybe that's why. And they whisked me in and out because they didn't want to get arrested. I bled for a month."

Maggie was patting her hand. "You're okay now."

"I know, I know. There's the pill now. But still . . . I just don't want to risk that again. It was too horrible."

"Of course not. None of us do."

"I was relieved, but . . . you know, kids and flowers. Ideals. I still get depressed every year on the anniversary. I wish it could have been different."

"I know." Maggie's eyes, too, were too bright.

Sue frowned at her fiercely. "So that's my story. Yours too?"

Maggie took a deep breath. "Near enough," she said. "Twice burned."

"Oh," said Sue.

"So I've had enough. From now on old Maggie toughs it alone."

"You don't envy Jackie?"

"Sure. Physically I do. Frank's damn good in bed. But it wasn't staying casual. So if they hit it off, hurray for both of them. I mean, Frank is a decent guy. And statistically her chances are pretty good. I've heard of several happy endings."

"What was wrong with him?"

"Nothing. That was the problem. I can't stand being vulnerable again. Even for someone decent."

"Not in control," said Mary Beth unexpectedly. She had been listening intently.

"Right." Maggie's attention switched to Mary Beth. "Maybe that's what we're all doing here. Getting back in control."

"But men are in control. You just said so."

"Not of everything. How can you say that?" demanded Sue, adding unfairly: "You started all this by dropping Tip. Does he control you?"

"Jeez, no! I never want to see him again." He had said, How could you do this to me?

"This, mind you," Sue said to Maggie, "is only a few months after as torrid an affair as you're likely to see in this uncensored century." Mary Beth covered her face. "Seriously, Swede, how can you say you're not in control? What the hell did Tip do to you?"

"Hey, easy," said Maggie, breaking in. "There are lots of ways to get hurt, Sue. When we're ready to give details we'll let you know."

"Closemouthed as the CIA," grumbled Sue, but, belatedly, she seemed to realize it was time to stop. She said, "Hey, is anyone else hungry?"

"Sure am," said Maggie. They all went to plunder the refrigerator. Mary Beth, as usual, had no appetite, but she managed to drink a cup of coffee.

The theatre tickets were for the first Wednesday in April. Late Tuesday night Mary Beth knocked on Maggie's bedroom door to announce that Ixil coffee was available, if she wanted, and found her sprawled on the floor reading Shakespeare. The closeted books had been unpacked, filling an empty shelf and even displacing a few math books.

"I just realized, I've never read *Titus Andronicus,*" said Maggie, faintly surprised. "Horrible play."

"I've managed to miss it too," smiled Mary Beth. "Along with several others."

"Well, I don't recommend it. It takes a strong stomach. Like your coffee. But I accept anyway." She stood up and followed Mary Beth into the hall. Mary Beth wanted to ask, Was he in theatre? But she had learned her lesson and held her tongue.

The production of *The Three Sisters* was mediocre. The young actress playing Masha was promising, but the others varied from satisfactory to clumsy. Still, the playwright's vision came through from time to time, and as usual Mary Beth found herself gratefully lost in it for the evening. It was one of her few joys, to immerse herself in another world, to suffer sorrows other than her own, to be taken out of herself, her dull and worthless self.

Afterward they stopped for a drink at the Steamboat. They sat in a booth under gingerbread woodwork, having an enjoyable debate about whether Chekhov really understood women. There was something a little odd in Maggie's mood, and Mary Beth finally identified it as relief. She too was pleased that her friend had exorcised whatever ghost had been troubling her. It was a good evening. Mary Beth felt almost back to normal. She had forced herself to relax.

Aqbal, that day of evil, had come and gone four times without hurting her. Things were getting better.

She met Maggie briefly in the hall that night on her way to the bathroom. "Hey, you okay?" she asked hopefully.

"A hundred percent," Maggie said. "Well, ninety-eight percent. Thanks, Mary Beth. For the push."

"I really didn't mean to," apologized Mary Beth.

"Maybe not. But it helped." Maggie flashed her wide grin and clapped Mary Beth lightly on the shoulder as she started on down the hall. "Hey, don't worry. I'm a swimmer too!"

VII
13 Qanil
(April 4, 1968)

She almost escaped, screaming and running back toward the ramp, but he caught her before anyone stopped, and walked her back down slowly, powerful in his anger. Important for things to look normal from the highway. But she was so frantic it was hard. Bitch. Trying to control him. Mum's hand gripping his ten-year-old arm, her ginny breath hissing, "Behave or I'll cut off your finger, I'll cut off your . . ." No. No more. Under the pilings, out of sight, he thought he had her. Her struggles fed his anger and his smothering hand quieted her. But then he lost it, and even though he tried a long time he couldn't get it back. Clumsy bitch. A lot of them were clumsy like that. As he stood up finally, she squirmed away, and he had to stab twice, once in the back, and once, sloppily, on the neck. Bitch.

But the triangle on the cheek was very precise and neat.

The only problem was that the kitten had come to and disappeared. Well, no matter, it would be hit by a car or something.

On April 4, Martin Luther King Jr. was assassinated. In a hundred cities across the U.S., riots boiled up—blind outpourings of violence in response to inexplicable violence. The symbol of peaceful racial change was dead, and so, it seemed, was peaceful change. Laconia was lucky. The south side, heavily black, poured into the streets in fury and was joined by swarms of university students, heavily white, and furious too. The downtown parks were trampled and many speeches were made, but only a few windows were broken in the frustrated grief and rage of the day.

Jane, standing on the edge of the crowd next to Roger, felt the helpless anger and sorrow as they listened to a black minister praying. She pulled her shawl tighter about her.

"God, Roger," she said in a low voice, "what can we do?"

"Nothing, hon. Sometimes there's just nothing we can do."

"I can't believe that."

"Sometimes things are just out of control."

"I am so damn mad at the world."

"Yeah."

She listened a moment more, then said, "Let's go home and get drunk."

"We're talking about the Ving Tsun system," said Ed Hamlin. "It was developed by a woman, and does not depend on physical strength alone. Quickness, yes. Lots of hard practice, yes. Skill doesn't come overnight. Today, I'll talk about staying out of trouble in the first place. Then we'll move on to the basic principles of Ving Tsun."

Ed was a dignified, cold-eyed young man. WAR had hired him for two demonstrations. Now he looked around the group in the large seminar room and said, "Okay, stand up, please. You and you."

He was indicating Jane and Sue Snyder. They both rose uncertainly.

"Two women, same height," said Ed. "Professor Freeman and . . . ?"

"Sue Snyder," said Sue.

"Okay. Sue, you're in much better shape to cope with an attack than Professor Freeman."

"Ha! Don't mess with me!" said Sue smugly.

"What's my problem?" asked Jane.

"Okay. Start at the top. Professor Freeman is wearing a chain around her neck." True; it held the little gold watch Roger had given her. "Bad choice. I know you're interested in rape especially, but robbery should be avoided too. In fact, sometimes it turns into rape. Jewelry like that is easily snatched, if the chain is weak; if it isn't, it could be used to strangle you."

"Okay," said Jane.

"Number two. Sue is wearing jeans. Not ideal, but pretty good

66

for mobility. Professor Freeman is in a skirt. Luckily skirts are pretty short now, but you can see how even the dress Professor Freeman is wearing can constrict movement in a fight. One of our basic moves is a front kick, and you'd have trouble."

"I have trouble even in jeans," said Sue, demonstrating.

"We'll fix that." Ed Hamlin moved on to the next topic, demonstrating basic stances and how to deflect blows and kicks. He was good, though Jane wondered despairingly if she'd ever learn to be quick enough. Constant work on a tenure dossier left little time for exercise, and she felt slow and clumsy next to Maggie or Terry.

By the time the Ving Tsun session was over, Jane was even further off schedule. Yesterday the computer had accepted her cards in a calm and competent whir, thought a moment, and then printed out, politely, the not very surprising news that there was an error somewhere. Now she wedged her door open and sat at her desk, the big manual before her. She began to compare the control cards with the instructions, letter by letter. But there were no mistakes. After the third careful check, Jane slammed the manual shut. "Goddamn imbecile machine!"

"Did I hear you mention a computer?"

Jane turned to the door. "Maggie! You work with that beast! Can you tell me what the hell it wants me to do?"

"I can try." Maggie set down her bookbag, looked at the printout message, and then compared Jane's control cards to the manual. "There," she said, pointing at the eleventh card.

"But that's correct!"

"You punched in comma-space instead of just comma."

"Oh God, you're right. That's the way humans always type it. How can you see things like that?"

Maggie shrugged. "I'm afflicted with a mind like a goddamn imbecile machine. I notice details—and gaps."

"Wish I had that affliction," grumbled Jane.

"Is this the analysis of your prelinguistic phonetic study?"

"Yes. Word gets around, doesn't it?"

Maggie picked up her bookbag. "My roommate's in your seminar. Jackie Edwards. She says your research is very exciting."

"Well, thanks. And thanks for explaining the damn computer."

"Sure." Maggie swung off down the hall. An interesting and competent young woman. Jane, gathering up her cards, thought that she'd like to get to know her better. After the tenure push was over, of course.

The computer terminals were housed in the basement, not far from the equipment room and labs, in a big fluorescent-lit room with small, high-set windows. There was a tinge of ozone in the air there, glaring white walls and tweedy gray commercial carpet, pale gray plastic tables. A hygienic modern design, marred only by the wastebaskets overflowing with discarded printouts, by the cardboard boxes clumsily arranged to hold more waste. The designer of the room had not counted on so much error. Clearly, he had never used a computer.

She had to wait her turn at a keypunch, but got the card right on the second try. She slipped it into the correct place in her pack and read it into the machine.

Almost immediately, the computer went down.

"What's happening?" she asked the attendant as he hung up the phone.

"I don't know. All the action is out at the CS lab."

"Did they say when it would be working again?"

"Couple of hours."

"Will I have to read in my cards again?"

"Nope. Not unless it's worse than they think."

"Okay. Guess I'll come back later, then."

As she climbed the stairs, she wondered how much time she had actually saved. With her calculator, she could have worked the statistical analysis in an hour or two. The computer did it in seconds, of course. But those seconds were surrounded by time at the keypunch, more time figuring out where the mistakes were, still more waiting for the machine to decide to function.

But of course if she did it herself she wouldn't produce all those reams of impressive wastepaper.

Her seminar topic today was the sound system of English. Jane, showing slides of the spectrograms of syllables like pa and ba, marveled as she always did at the subtleties humans could discern. Even very small humans, as young as Linc's son. As young as little Greg? Well, the computer would tell her soon. She hoped.

After class, she checked her mailbox to find a note from the chairman. He announced proudly that he had been appointed to a national policy review task force by someone in the Johnson administration. He would therefore be away frequently during the next six weeks. While the department was honored by the appointment, et cetera, et cetera, it meant that certain important departmental decisions, including tenure recommendations, would have to be delayed. Early June, he promised. Damn. Damn, damn, damn! Would this tension ever be over?

Already despondent, she went back down to the computer room. Her printout was waiting in a big stack of completed jobs. She pulled it out and unfolded it. Thank God, it had run this time. But as she read on down the pages, her heart sank. There were the means, the numbers neatly arrayed in exactly the order she had predicted. A beautiful confirmation of her hypothesis.

Except that the statistics showed that it was not significant. It didn't count. There was so much random variation among those individualistic babies that the differences she was looking for might have been accidental. The fast habituators and the slow habituators had canceled out the effects of the change of syllables, made them look unimportant.

So. That was it. Scratch the last four months' work. Scratch tenure too? Perhaps.

Depressed, she took the sheets and went to see Josh. The loading door that led from the equipment room to the parking lot was open, and in a moment Josh appeared. He was humming tunelessly, happily. His radio was playing, but he was humming something else.

"Hi, Josh."

"Oh, hi, Jane. Got a printout?"

"Yes."

"Just let me get this tachistoscope out of the way." He went up the stepladder and stowed the equipment carefully on a shelf.

"It washed out," said Jane as he came down.

"Oh, really?" He smiled broadly.

"Josh, are you stoned?"

"Just a nice little buzz. I'm okay. Let's see it."

She spread out the relevant pages. "It's the variation among the subjects that killed it."

He looked at it, still humming, and finally said, "Yeah. Tough."

"So, we start over, I guess."

"Yeah. But look at those fantastic means!"

She wondered if he were seeing them in Technicolor. She said, "Right. But they're not statistically significant."

"Yeah, but look. All we have to do is get a few more of those kids to habituate, right? Let's make the preliminary habituation tape a loop."

"A loop. So instead of having a fixed time for habituation, we have a fixed level of habituation."

"Right! We can keep the loop going for thirty minutes if we have to. Then when the kid has settled down we switch to the stimulus tape. I can rig that easily. I'll get you a second tape recorder. That one right there." He pointed to a shiny metal machine on the shelves above.

"Okay. Good idea, Josh. I'll go figure out what to use for the habituation criterion." The twenty-four babies she had just tested in vain would at least be useful for deciding on that.

"Okay, great."

Jane sighed. "I just hate to be starting all over."

"Hey, but listen, it'll work this time! Just look at those means!"

She said, "Okay. Thanks, Josh. You get the recorder down. I'll go start collecting babies. Week after next okay?"

"Yeah. Great!"

As she plodded down the hall she heard him return to his tuneless tune. Maybe he had the right idea. She slipped into the women's room and took a Valium. But she still didn't feel like singing. Maybe she ought to ask Josh what he was on. The means, when she looked at them again, remained depressingly black and white.

An hour later she had finished redesigning the experiment, had chosen the most appropriate criterion level for habituation, and was turning to her file of birth records. Jane's secretary was amused that her job required clipping birth announcements from the paper every day. "You ought to send them all congratulations," she had said once, as she handed Jane the week's collection of announcements.

"Yeah, like the draft, you mean. Aunt Jane wants you!"

"Right!"

Now Jane sifted through the clippings, pulling out the birth announcements of babies who would be three months old week after next. She noted down the parents' names and addresses and turned to the telephone directory.

There was a knock on her open door. She looked up. "Hi, Linc. What can I do for you?"

Linc, looking haggard, stepped in. "Nothing, I guess. Hold my hand."

"Chairman's note? No decisions till June? Damn frustrating."

"More than that. My heredity paper just came back. Viciously unfair reviewer."

"You can send it to another journal."

"Yeah. I'll try. But nobody'll accept it soon enough."

"I know. Boy, do I know."

He sat down heavily, huge in the little straight chair, and frowned a little. "You mean you're having trouble too?"

She waved a hand at the offending printout. "Washout. Thirty tedious babies, six thrown out for various reasons, the usable ones too variable. All thirty down the drain."

"God, I'm sorry, Jane."

"Well, it happens. We'll both recover."

"Yeah. I guess. Hal was just asked to do a book chapter."

"Damn."

"Yeah. It's a hell of a time for us to get hit with this."

"Right. Psychologically bad, as we experts say."

He grinned at her suddenly. "Yeah."

"Will you have to change your paper much for the next journal?"

"Not really. I thought I could change the introductory paragraph a little, maybe. Put in a couple of references to articles in that journal."

"Good PR."

"Yeah." His eyes were dark and grateful. "How about you, Jane? Is it really a total loss?"

"No. Wish it were, it might be less frustrating. But it came out exactly as predicted. Except there was so much individual variation that my test says, correctly, that it might all be chance."

"Mm. I see. But really, it's good to know you're on the right track."

"Oh, yes, theoretically that's true. I'm just not ready to face thirty more damn babies."

Linc laughed. "Just listen to us," he said. He got up and kicked the wedge from under her door so that it would close. "We're two educated, brilliant, adult human beings, completely routed by thirty infants and a flock of finches."

Jane smiled. "True. Listen, Linc, could you leave the door open? I get kind of edgy with it closed."

He took her hand and pulled her up, suddenly serious. "Jane, I just wanted to say thanks. You're the only person around here who can really understand me."

71

"Linc, don't be silly."

"But it's true. You can be honest and still never hurt." His hands were moving up her arms, tenderly. Jesus, thought Jane, here it comes, my wife doesn't understand me, let's comfort each other.

She pushed against his chest. "Linc, okay, that's enough."

"Jane, please. Be honest. You must feel something too, you're always so sensitive to me."

His face was closer now but it seemed farther away. The walls were closing in, throbbing at her. She had to get out, get out, so she could breathe. She closed her eyes, felt a ballpoint pen on the desk behind her, and jabbed Linc with it blindly.

There was a knock on the door.

"Come in!" cried Jane desperately. Linc, his face twisted with pain, released her suddenly. She fell back against the desk, half-sitting.

The door opened and the room stopped throbbing. Her student Jackie Edwards stood there, accompanied by a tall young man with a swatch of dark hair falling across his forehead.

"Oh, I'm sorry, Professor Freeman. I didn't mean to interrupt."

"No problem, Jackie. Professor Berryman had finished."

"Right," said Linc, successfully hiding most of the hurt in his voice. "See you later, Jane."

"Cheers."

As he left, his eyes met Jackie's knowing ones briefly. God, I hope she's discreet, thought Jane. No sense getting Cathy Berryman upset. Unbidden, another thought intruded into her mind. Thank God, thank God it was Linc, and not someone who would be voting on tenure.

She forced herself to become businesslike. "Well, what can I do for you, Jackie?"

"I just realized that last week's reserve reading would really be useful for my paper, but someone else has it checked out now. Would it be possible to borrow yours? I could copy it on the basement machine, and have it back in ten minutes."

"Sure, Jackie. The Gibson paper?"

"Yes. I wouldn't bother you, but the paper's due in three weeks and I may have to visit my subjects again to check some things Gibson says."

Jane pulled out the mimeographed sheets, wrote "Gibson—

72

J. Edwards" on a slip of paper, and handed the folder to Jackie. "There you go," she said.

"Thanks. I'll bring it right back." She and her handsome escort headed for the stairs.

Jane replaced the wedge under her door. God, what a day. What a week. She went back to her list of happy new parents and began to look up telephone numbers.

Across the nation, the rioting went on.

VIII

6 Kaoo
(June 14, 1968)

Robert Kennedy had been the next to go. The university was rocked by the tragic news just as the first summer session began. Sue's summer work kept her on campus all day, but Jackie and Mary Beth and Maggie came back from their shorter duties to watch the TV glumly.

Sirhan Sirhan was arrested immediately and soon Dr. King's assassin was found too. "Well, at least they're starting to catch the guys," said Jackie.

"Justice triumphant," said Maggie bitterly.

So it was a refreshing change, a few days later, when Jackie and Frank returned from an afternoon date in Syracuse with something pleasant to report.

"It was so wonderful, and so sad," Jackie enthused. "Wasn't it, Frank?"

"It was terrific," he agreed.

"I cried and cried. You really ought to go see it."

"Wish I could," said Sue. They were all sitting on the square front porch, enjoying the fresh silky June night and trying to ignore the music throbbing from across the street.

"Where is this place?" asked Mary Beth.

"Just outside of Syracuse. I guess it used to be a farm, but they have a real theatre building now."

"There's no way you can go?" Mary Beth asked Sue.

"Nope. Too far, too long. This weekend I'm supposed to be charming hostess and interpreter to a couple of Russian professors visiting the chemistry department. And I can't afford the time anyway until this goddamn summer session is over.''

"*Cyrano* will be closed by then," said Jackie regretfully. "But they're doing a bunch of other shows this summer."

Mary Beth looked hopefully at Maggie. The good-natured blue eyes met hers a moment. "Sure," said Maggie. "I love *Cyrano* too. But I promised Jackie here she could use my car this weekend while I'm fixing the brakes on hers."

"We'll take the Land Rover," said Mary Beth, delighted.

And so Friday night, the fourteenth of June, they drove the forty minutes through the scent of new clover to the Syracuse farm that housed the theatre, Mary Beth in a pale yellow dress with her Nebaj woven belt, Maggie in light blue and white stripes. There was one odd moment on the way. Maggie had asked, "Do you know anything about this production?"

"Just what Jackie said. The scenery is a bit simplified, but the costumes and everything are good."

"Who are the actors?"

"I forget his name, but the guy doing Cyrano is really good, she said. I think it's your usual summer stock company, good professional actors who aren't superfamous, plus young new ones."

"Mm."

"Jackie gave me her program. If you're interested it's in the outside pocket of my bag there."

Maggie pulled out the folded program and flipped it open. Suddenly she said violently, "Goddamn it, Mary Beth!"

"What?"

"What the hell are you trying to do?"

She was genuinely angry. Mary Beth glanced at her, bewildered. "What do you mean?"

Maggie checked herself visibly. "You don't know?"

"No, I don't know. What are you talking about?"

Maggie didn't answer, just leaned back in the passenger seat and stared out the window for a moment at the young green world. Eventually Mary Beth said, "Well, whatever it is, I apologize."

"Oh, what the hell." Maggie sounded cheerful again. "Let's forget it and just enjoy the goddamn play."

They did. The theatre was well equipped technically, although the wooden seats were not the most comfortable in the world. The director handled the crowd scenes skillfully. Roxane and Christian were suitably beautiful, and Cyrano, as Jackie had promised, was splendid. The long hideous nose was the only flaw in this twinkling muscular soldier with the enchanting flexible voice and sorrowful brown eyes. The poetry, the swordplay, the intense pain of his unrequited love were all woven flawlessly into the romantic fabric of the show. As the lights came up afterward Mary Beth was still pressing her handkerchief to her face, and she thought Maggie's eyes too were suspiciously shiny. They moved slowly with the crowd up the aisle toward the exit.

"That was so good!" Mary Beth said when she could speak.

"Yes."

"Jackie was absolutely right."

"Yes."

"That actor was really good, wasn't he?"

"Yes."

"God, I wonder how he does it."

"Talent and hard work, I imagine." There was an ironic edge in Maggie's voice. But Mary Beth was too enthusiastic to stop.

"He was really good," she said again.

"Yes." And then, carelessly, Maggie added, "You want to go congratulate him?"

"Oh, no, he's probably busy now. He wouldn't appreciate people popping in."

"They'll do it anyway. And why wouldn't he appreciate it?"

"It would be nice to meet him," said Mary Beth wistfully. "But . . ."

"Then come on." With sudden resolution Maggie pushed out of the lobby door and turned abruptly to the side, skimming around the building and back toward the stage door so swiftly that Mary Beth had to run a few steps to keep up. No one stopped them. They found themselves in a narrow hall. Mary Beth regretted her whim now. What could they say to an actor that he hadn't already heard a thousand times? But Maggie, unstoppable, stuck her head into a crowded room where actors and many other people were chattering excitedly. "Where's Cyrano?" she asked a young man near the door.

He pointed farther along the hall. "First door around the corner," he said cheerfully. Maggie nodded and followed directions.

He was in the hall by his open door, his broad back to them, talking to a couple of other people. Maggie paused several feet away from them, and Mary Beth sensed suddenly that she was tense too, very tense, like an athlete prepared for a difficult test. Damn, why

76

were they here? The actor was still in tights and loose white shirt and full makeup, including the long nose. Dark hair curled from the loosened cuffs of the shirt, but his head was balding. He was holding his stiff white ruff in his hand. He was a big, solid man; seeing him now, Mary Beth was a little surprised at the agility he had shown on stage, the ease and grace with which he had performed the sword fights and the leaps onto tables or ramparts.

The well-dressed couple he was talking to smiled and finished congratulating him, then turned to go. Maggie said, in a low clear voice, "In fact, ladies and gentlemen, the actual underlying nose is a trifle bumpy but rather nice."

He turned, and Mary Beth had never seen such an expression of pure joy as the one that lit his friendly face. "Mademoiselle Marguerite!" he exclaimed; and it was apparently the right thing to say because Maggie relaxed a little, smiling too, in the instant before he had bounded across to wrap her in an immense hug. Then suddenly he seemed to have second thoughts and stepped back a little, still holding her hands but pushing her to arm's length, the warm brown eyes searching her face anxiously.

"You're okay," he said.

"Sure." She shrugged. "You too?"

"Getting that way." He smiled a little. They were both ignoring Mary Beth. He said, "I've thought about you, Maggie. But I was a little afraid to meet."

Maggie smiled a little too, and nodded.

Mary Beth said, "So was she."

"Yes, well, we'd been through a lot." He glanced at her, accepting her as naturally as though she belonged, and then turned back to Maggie. "It's so damn good to see you!" he said, amazement still clear in his voice.

"Yeah." She was still smiling at him, pleased and relieved now, not tense. Then she remembered and said, "Nick, here's one of my very best friends. Mary Beth Nelson. Mary Beth, this is Nick O'Connor. Uncle Nick."

"Hi, Mary Beth." He shook her hand.

"Hi. I thought you were terrific tonight," she faltered, not quite knowing what to say. But he beamed at her as though he had never been complimented before.

"Thanks. It's a terrific play."

"Un succès fou," said Maggie.

He looked at the two of them with enormous pleasure and said,

"Look, come in while I get off my nose. Then we'll go have some coffee." He motioned toward the dressing room behind him and then cleared bits of costume off a couple of folding chairs for them. As he sat down by the mirror, he said again to Maggie, "Hey, you're okay."

"Sure," she said. "It was only my elbow."

He grinned conspiratorially at Mary Beth. "Only her elbow! Last time I saw her she was strapped up in the flashiest sling you ever saw. Gorgeous. Probably designed by Dior. But Maggie, I never did quite understand how you hurt yourself."

She was smiling at him again. "Stupid trick on the uneven bars," she explained. "Got myself too tired and twisted my arm on the dismount. I've been a lot more careful since."

"Good. It looked pretty painful."

"Doesn't hurt at all now. But I've sworn off that particular stunt."

"I see. But you know, human beings are pretty resilient," he said. He turned to the mirror and began, carefully, to remove the grotesque nose. "Time heals, they say."

"That certainly is what they say," agreed Maggie neutrally. In the mirror Mary Beth could see that his friendly brown eyes had flicked to Maggie's image. Then he asked her what she was doing now, and they talked about the university and about statistics and about WAR for a few minutes.

He was slapping cold cream all over his face and down his neck and even on top of his balding head, Mary Beth noticed, and down into the edges of the little beard and all over his hands and hairy forearms. Then he wiped it off carefully with tissues. The nose took a little more attention. "Hate this spirit gum," he complained, rubbing alcohol on it.

"One of the few roles he can't do with his own face," Maggie said.

His own face, as it was gradually revealed, was reassuringly ordinary, pleasantly ugly, an average guy with a little beard. Well, not quite average. His eyes were clear brown and filled with light, like water moving over rocks. Mary Beth suddenly realized that he was watching her reflection as she watched him. The lively eyes met hers briefly in the mirror, and she looked away guiltily.

"Sorry," murmured Mary Beth in confusion.

"Hey, it's okay," he said.

"He likes being watched," explained Maggie. "Actors do."

"Right." He was amused.

"It's just that you look so different," Mary Beth explained.

He grinned at her. "Thank God. Cyrano's the only guy I know who's uglier than I am."

"Well, I don't mean just the nose. I mean the person."

Serious now, he turned around in his chair and nodded at her. "You're right," he said. "It's a funny process, getting in and out of makeup and costume. It isn't just surface, it's a whole personality that's being put on and taken off."

"It must be odd," she said. She wished she could take off her personality that easily, put on the old confident Mary Beth again.

"I suppose it is. I'm used to it." He looked suddenly merry. "Let me tell you my nightmare. Every now and then, if you're seriously distracted on stage, you lose the character for a minute. Your lines are just recited until you find yourself again. Well, the nightmare is that it happens in reverse. I take off my ruff and my nose and there's no Nick there. Just air."

"Like Peer Gynt's onion," said Maggie, amused.

"Exactly! Peel off all the surface layers to find the kernel, and there's nothing there."

"No danger," said Maggie reassuringly. "You've got character to spare."

"Well, thanks. But doesn't it make a good nightmare?"

"Excellent. I think you'd worry about something else too, though."

"What's that?"

"Suppose you took off your nose and put on your jeans and then found out you were still Cyrano? A short-nosed Cyrano?"

He laughed. "That might be fun. But I'd hate to have it happen in some other plays."

"He makes an excellent villain too," Maggie explained to Mary Beth.

"Hey, look," said Nick. "I'm going to get into the aforementioned jeans and then we'll go somewhere. It'll take me about a minute. Okay?"

Maggie stood up. "We'll wait in the hall."

"Okay. Or you could go inspect the stage if you want."

"Oh, I'd love to!" said Mary Beth. "But we don't know anything about it."

"We might fall down a trap," said Maggie, smiling at her. "But maybe Nick could give us a quick tour in a minute."

"Always glad to give a hand to trembling, moist-eyed, helpless females," he said, and knew to duck as Maggie, laughing, swung at him. She and Mary Beth went into the hall.

"Why didn't you tell me?" Mary Beth asked urgently when his door had closed.

Maggie shrugged. "Didn't know I'd ever see him again."

Mary Beth frowned at her. "You knew in the car. There's more to it than that."

"Yes. But not that I can talk about."

Mary Beth was silent. Some things should not be talked about, true. But how could there by anything to hide about the big comfortable balding man in the dressing room?

"You said uncle," she said tentatively at last.

"An honorary title."

"He is sort of like an uncle."

"Mm-hmm," said Maggie. The door opened and Nick, now transformed into an average American with a little beard and jeans and plaid shirt, joined them. Maggie added, to him, "You'll be Mary Beth's honorary uncle too, won't you, Nick?"

"Sure. Any friend of yours is a niece of mine."

"Great. Listen, we really would like to look around the theatre."

"Okay. Let's see. You must have passed the greenroom on the way in."

"Yes."

"We'll skip that, then. Step right this way, folks, through the amazing incredible scene shop, noted in song, story, and commercial. E.g.: Edna, my flats are not as white as yours, what is your secret? Well, Marge, I got mine at the Syracuse Farm Theatre." Even his falsetto could assume different personalities. Laughing, Maggie and Mary Beth followed him into a large many-storied room lined with stacks of platforms and racks of tall canvas flats, then through half of a huge double door. It was dark here; Mary Beth was aware of tall velour curtains and an array of ropes along the wall beside her. There were a few lights high up among the pipes and ropes that seemed to rise to a dusty infinity above her. Maggie stepped between a couple of the curtains and stood looking up, shading her eyes, the light blue and white dress a glimmer in the shadows. Nick watched her a moment, then glanced at Mary Beth.

"Have you been backstage before?" he asked.

80

"Only in high school. And that was really just the gym with a curtain."

He grinned. "I know what you mean. Started out in that sort of place myself. Acting to an audience that ate peanuts and flew paper airplanes. Well, okay. Come on out here." He led the way to Maggie's side, and Mary Beth realized that they were standing in the first act setting for *Cyrano,* the little toy stage in front of her, the arches at the side. It looked strange and flat. She turned to ask him a question, but he was watching Maggie again. Feeling extraneous, Mary Beth feigned interest in the little fake stage and walked away from them for a moment to study it. She was not far enough, though, to avoid hearing him ask softly, "Maggie. How is your heart?"

Mary Beth tensed, half expecting a lashing out, one of the stinging replies that she and Sue had received for such meddling. But instead Maggie replied quietly in French, *"On se debrouille. Et toi?"*

"I'm coping too."

"Good." And then, cheerfully, she called, "Mary Beth, come look at the flies. See? The whole show is up there."

"Where?"

Nick pointed up. "There's the pastry shop, and right behind it is the cloister."

She squinted, and could dimly make out the flat canvas sets in the murky realms above.

"Hey," Maggie exclaimed, "enough of this painted garbage! Where's the electrical stuff?"

"Still like lights best?"

"Of course. You actors would be nothing without lights."

"Rule one for actors," said Nick to Mary Beth. "Never offend the lighting crew. Their revenge is too horrible to contemplate." He waved his hand toward the wings. "The auxiliary board is there by the stage manager's desk."

Maggie crossed the stage and studied it with interest. "Main board up in the back of the house?"

"Yes. You want to go up there?"

"If it's not too much for your old bones."

They started toward the auditorium through a curtain by the stage manager's little desk. Maggie stopped abruptly in the tiny hall beyond. "Sound system?" she asked.

81

"Yes. Or at least it was. One of the speakers is on the blink. They were using a little backup outfit tonight."

"Yeah, I thought the sound wasn't up to the standards of the rest of the show."

They were looking at a set of huge loudspeakers, and a piece of electronic equipment. "Did they check the amp?" asked Maggie, poking a finger at it delicately.

"I don't know. They seldom consult me. Can't imagine why."

"Bet I could fix it."

"Bet you could too. A most acute juvenal."

He led the way up a little flight of stairs to the light booth. "Hi, Bruce," he said to the bearded young man in it. "Friends of mine want to see the booth."

"Sure," said Bruce.

Maggie stepped in and said, "Hey, terrific!"

"Is it good?" asked Mary Beth, peering around her. Nick lounged against the door frame, watching them, unhurried.

"Yes, this is what we were going to buy if a rich donor ever gave the Hargate theatre any money." Maggie was engrossed in reading a complicated chart with mysterious penciled instructions. She put the papers down and looked in satisfaction at the panel of switches. "You're preset for Act One," she said.

"Right," said Bruce.

"Could I show my friend the first cue?"

Bruce glanced back at Nick, who nodded. "I guess so," said Bruce. "You turn the board on over there, and . . ." But she had already switched on the board and killed the work lights that had been on backstage. Mary Beth looked out the booth window, fascinated, as Maggie slid levers around and the Act One set sprang to life, the spattered flat canvas they had inspected a moment ago suddenly turning into Cyrano's little theatre.

Nick was watching now too. He said, "Looks good. Never saw it from up here."

"Let's see where you enter," said Maggie, glancing at the card in front of her and reaching for a lever. "It's a three-count, right, Bruce?"

"Yes. Just count a thousand and one, a thousand and two, a thousand and three."

"The thousands are to make sure you don't get excited and count too fast," Maggie explained to Mary Beth.

"I always preferred to count one-chimpanzee, two-chimpanzee," said Nick. "More interesting."

"Friend of mine from North Carolina claimed that down there they count one-watermelon, two-watermelon," Maggie said evenly. Bruce chuckled.

"Someone ought to do a study," said Nick. "Publishable, don't you think? . . . 'Dialect Variations in Lighting Counts.' "

Maggie turned to him, laughing with the others. "Great idea," she agreed. "Now watch." The light on the side steps increased and Mary Beth remembered, yes, the long-nosed Frenchman had first entered just there.

"Want a job?" Bruce asked Maggie.

She smiled at him. "No, thanks. I'm pretty busy already."

"You've run lights before."

"Designed 'em, hung 'em, run 'em, cussed 'em," she said. "But now I only do consulting work." She had returned the board to its original condition, and now turned it off and switched the work lights back on.

"Got too many consultants already," grumbled Bruce.

"Yeah, I always thought so too. Thanks, Bruce. Good job tonight." She went out of the lighting booth and looked at Nick. "Hey, I'm glad I came," she said.

He said, "You haven't been backstage for a while."

"Not for a year." He nodded soberly, and she added, "But it turns out to be fun, Nick. It's a wonderful world."

"Yes."

"You still game for coffee?"

"More than ever."

"Let's go, then."

IX

6 Kaoo
(June 14, 1968)

His car led the Land Rover to a little country restaurant with knotty pine walls and furniture and curtains done in red calico. The waitresses had frilly aprons. Other actors were there already, and the one who had played Christian waved at them. "Hey, Nick! Bring your poppets over here and join us!"

Nick turned to them inquiringly, but Maggie had already put on a poppet face for Christian and was gushing, "Oh, thank you, but Mr. O'Connor is already more than we two li'l gals can manage."

Nick grinned and took them to a booth in the rear. They ordered pie and coffee. Then he leaned back and regarded Maggie with satisfaction. "Your mother," he said.

"What about my mother?"

"Last time I saw you, you and your elbow were going home to campaign for her."

"Oh, right. She won."

"She's mayor of Owensboro now," said Mary Beth proudly.

"Terrific!"

"Yeah. She's good. Lucky town," said Maggie.

"What'll she do next? Senator or something?"

"I don't think so. She's happier at the local level because she hears from more people. It's so easy to get insulated at the national level, lose touch with what people want us to stand for."

"What a world! It's all in knots right now."

"It always is, somewhere," said Mary Beth morosely.

"Yeah. Thank God for music and theatre," said Maggie. "Otherwise I'd give up." After a moment she added musingly, "Sure hope they get your sound system fixed."

"They seemed stuck. Said we'd have to limp along with the little outfit for a while." He was watching her alertly.

"Maybe they should send it out to be fixed."

"To the electrical hospital." As their eyes met, Mary Beth felt that they were saying something else.

"Exactly," said Maggie. "Pie isn't bad," she added with satisfaction, popping a forkful of cherries into her mouth. "How's yours, Swede?"

"Good." Mary Beth had chosen strawberry-rhubarb. "And the coffee's good too." It was strong and hot.

"Thank you," said Nick.

"Haven't you had enough applause tonight?" chided Maggie. "You're taking credit for the coffee too?"

"Damn right," said Nick. "Me and the Syracuse Farm Theatre Company. We trained the chef."

"Ah."

"Well, what sort of coffee do you think they'd have here?"

Maggie glanced at a frilly apron passing by and wrinkled her nose.

"Right," he said. "That's what it was. But we had a conference after the first day and swore solemnly to send back all weak coffee. We divided ourselves into good policemen and bad policemen."

Maggie's eyes were dancing. "Bad ones swore at them. Good ones said sweetly what a fine restaurant this was, but they sure wished they could get some espresso like Mama used to make."

"Right. And after three days of this treatment a good policeman finally got a good cup. We all cheered and he tipped heavily. It's been okay ever since."

"You were a bad policeman."

"Oh, yes, I was incredibly bad." A look of ineffable evil passed across his face. "Maidens quaked and strong men blushed when I darkened these doors. But I've reformed." He hung his head a little, the lucid eyes mournful with mock penitence. Maggie grinned at him.

"What a useful project!"

"Yes, I thought so. I figure it did more for posterity than our *Cyrano* ever could. The O'Connor route to personal immortality."

"Ambitious man, isn't he?" Maggie said to Mary Beth. Then

she looked back at him thoughtfully. "Is that something you think about, Nick?"

"A little. More than I did." They were serious again. "I wouldn't change anything about theatre, of course. But it's always a little frustrating to know that in a few days it will disappear without a ripple."

She nodded. "That always made me sad too. To work so hard and even successfully, and then have it all disappear forever."

"Like painting the Mona Lisa, showing it to a few friends, and then burning it."

"But there are other ways of disappearing," Mary Beth said. "The Mayan stelae are carved in stone. But when the whole culture is wiped out, there's no one to appreciate it. I mean, we gringos go look at the ruins and feel very impressed. But it's not like the *Cyrano* tonight, when we understood the significance of every little gesture and every moment. We are impressed because we appreciate all those moments. With the Mayan things, we are impressed too but we can't really appreciate them."

Nick nodded. "That's the advantage of theatre, of course. It's constantly renewed. Always has a chance of communicating directly with the audience."

"Yes, I know," Maggie chimed in. "Live music and live theatre, that's when I believe in humanity."

"Yeah." He was pleased, oddly flattered.

"However," she added briskly, "if you want your contributions to last forever, go into math. Discover some eternal truth or other."

"Hey! Great idea. I'll do that first thing tomorrow."

"The Ryan route to personal immortality." They were grinning at each other again.

"There's always children," said Mary Beth. Maggie kicked her under the table. Hard.

"Yes, there are other possibilities," Nick said steadily, and Maggie relaxed again. "For example, I've been thinking about Hargate a lot this last year. I loved teaching the grads, and I've been trying to think why it was so important to me. The really top priority is to let people have that experience, whatever it is, that happens between actors and audience. Exactly what I'm doing now. But when I watched my students working on the skills that my mime teacher taught me, I felt connected, somehow. Attached to the past and the future. It was a very heady experience for a fly-by-night actor like me.''

"Passing the torch."

"The great relay race of life. Yeah. It's exciting in a very different way from the high I get on stage."

Maggie looked at Mary Beth. "The Ixil calendar," she said.

"I was thinking of that too," said Mary Beth. "Or the weaving." His brow wrinkled inquiringly, and she explained, "The people I'm studying are the Ixil in the highlands of Guatemala. They're poor and illiterate and isolated. But they've kept big hunks of Mayan culture alive despite the Conquest and the bloodshed since. Passing it on orally. Some very complicated things, like their calendar."

"So in fact the culture lives on?"

"No, it was destroyed as a culture. They can't read those stelae either. But parts of the culture, the skills, are not all gone. You can't erase time, they say. They've just added in things the Spaniards and gringos have forced on them, disguised just enough to be acceptable to the conquerors. So a lot of the Mayan themes are still there."

He nodded, satisfied. "So the old folk who knew the calendar managed to pass on the knowledge, despite the odds. I'd settle for that. I'd be proud to think that maybe four hundred years from now, or even forty, an actor was doing something that I had helped pass along. The O'Connor eye-roll." He demonstrated.

"Then why aren't you teaching now?" asked Maggie.

"Well, George has kept me very busy. My agent," he explained to Mary Beth. "It's been good for me, this year. Necessary, even. But one of these days I'm going to check out some schools. I don't want to stop acting, just add some teaching."

"I bet you're dabbling in it now."

He grinned. "Well, the young sprats in the company know I like to give out free advice," he admitted. "Windy O'Connor, everybody's uncle."

Maggie smiled at him fondly, sipping her coffee, then said almost idly, "I suppose everybody's uncle gets to have a key to the theatre."

Without hesitation, he pulled out a key ring and removed one, dropping it onto the table before him. "I don't use it often," he said. "It's to the stage door, and people are usually there already when I arrive at five."

She glanced around. "Do you suppose they'd bring us some more coffee? Your one sure gift to posterity? Of which Mary Beth and I represent the vanguard?"

He laughed and waved at the waitress, who brought it promptly. Maggie swallowed a little and turned to Mary Beth. "Hey, I've left something in the Land Rover I want to show to Nick. Could I have your key a minute?"

"Sure." Mary Beth handed it to her.

"I'll be right back." She disappeared. Nick gazed after her, amused. They were fond of each other, these two.

"Does she still set up a lot of pranks?" he asked.

"Pranks? Not really. I guess there were the alarm clocks."

"Alarm clocks?"

She told him, and he seemed very pleased. "I'm glad she decided to come see the play," he said.

"She didn't."

"What do you mean?" He looked at her, suddenly intent. Mary Beth hesitated. She didn't want to make any mistakes. But there was no graceful way to find out.

"Look," she said, "were you her lover?"

"Good Lord, no!" He was astonished, and Mary Beth relaxed a little. But he seemed perturbed by the question, and glanced back at the door where Maggie had disappeared before he turned back, frowning, to Mary Beth. "She said you were one of her best friends," he said.

"Yes. I guess I am."

"She wouldn't suggest a thing like that. So it must be she doesn't talk about it at all."

"She only said she was recovering from the cliché unhappy affair and didn't want to talk about it."

"I see." He picked up the saltshaker and turned it in his powerful well-trained hands, squinting at the patterns of light. Then he put it down. "Okay, look. I'm not going to say anything about her business. But I think I can safely explain my own presence in her life." Mary Beth nodded, grateful, and he went on. "I taught at Hargate for a term, and she was doing lights for the theatre there."

"She never mentioned that before tonight. This is only the second time this year she's even gone to see a play. And I dragged her to both of them."

"Hell. Did she know I was in this one?"

88

"Not till we were halfway here. Then she blistered my ears cursing, till she saw I didn't know about you."

"I see." He poked at the saltshaker again, then went on. "Anyway, when I met Maggie, I was married. And then my wife died."

"Oh God, I'm sorry." Mary Beth was appalled at her blundering. There's always children, she had said. She wanted to disappear.

But he continued, still friendly. "Maggie helped me so much then, when I was completely stunned and confused. She ignored her own problems and stood by. She helped pull me through. We've been through an awful lot together."

"But you didn't want to see each other."

"No. Everything was still so painful and raw when we saw each other last. I think we were both afraid of hurting the other one. Bringing back those terrible days."

"So it was more than just her elbow."

"Let's not get into her business." Friendly but firm. He could keep a trust.

"Tonight neither one of you seems hurt," she said after a moment.

"God, no! I guess our fears were groundless. When I saw her the only thing I felt was joy."

"The worries came back a minute later."

"Yes, observant friend. But not for long." He smiled at her.

"She was happy to see you."

"Yes, thank God. She's a more important friend to me than I'd realized."

Mary Beth glanced at the door where Maggie had disappeared. "What's taking her so long?" she asked.

Before he could answer, Christian appeared at their table.

"You've lost one of them, Nick," he said, smiling at Mary Beth.

"They slip through my fingers like quicksilver," said Nick. "Mary Beth, this is Cal Henderson."

"Hello."

"Hi, Mary Beth. Hope you're enjoying this country life."

"The play was wonderful," she said.

He beamed. "Nick, what good taste your friends have! Look, we're going across the street to the bar for a while. Why don't you bring Mary Beth and that other lovely creature if you find her, and we'll all have a beer?"

"I'll see what they say," said Nick. "Thanks."

"Good. See you, Mary Beth." Cal went away.

Nick looked back at Mary Beth and said, "You don't like that idea."

She was tense, clutching her handbag in her lap. "No, I . . . well, I prefer coffee to beer."

"Okay. No problem. Cal has plenty of other company." He didn't probe, just leaned back in the booth with a friendly grin, and said, "You're studying the Maya, you said. Are you an anthropologist?"

"A linguist," she said, relaxing a little, and they talked about the Ixil for a while until Maggie reappeared.

"Back at last," she said cheerfully, handing the keys to Mary Beth and sliding back into the booth.

"I've been learning about the Ixil," said Nick. "Did you know about the dance dramas?"

"The faithless wife and the seven Spaniards?"

"Yes, that's one. I find that inspiring. A people who have been devastated that way, learning to laugh about it. Somehow you feel that the inner core is still intact. They'll be going strong after we've disappeared."

"They emphasize learning to bear things. To endure," said Mary Beth. Jeez, why couldn't she endure? She turned to Maggie. "Hey, did you find what you were looking for?"

"Yes. But then I decided I should show Nick in the daylight. Are you busy Sunday, Nick?"

"Yes, early show. But I'm completely free Monday."

"Great! I'm done after my morning class. How about a picnic for lunch?"

"Yes. Where?"

"Litchfield Gorge. It's near the Schellsburg exit, about halfway to our house. That way nobody will have to drive too far."

"Done."

"But we'd better leave pretty soon tonight. It's a forty-minute drive from here," she explained.

"I'm glad you came," he said.

"I am too, Nick. It's all Mary Beth's doing."

Mary Beth suddenly found herself basking in the approving gaze of the brown eyes and the blue. She shrugged. "Guess I'm the fool who rushes in," she said.

Maggie grinned. "The angel too, as it turns out."

90

The waitress appeared with the check and they split it. Then Maggie stood up. "Is noon okay Monday?"

"Fine," said Nick.

"In the main parking lot. We walk up from there."

"Fine. I'll expect a full diagnosis."

"You'll have it. And there'll be other things to talk about too."

"I thought as much." They grinned at each other, and Mary Beth, puzzled, wondered what diagnosis he meant.

They were outside now in the satiny June air. A man came out from the bar across the street toward them, staggering a little. They slowed to let him pass in front of them toward the brightly lit parking lot.

"Nick, are you here for the whole summer?" asked Maggie.

"No, they just jobbed me in for *Cyrano*. I'll be off to the city again next week for a soap."

"Oh, will we be able to see you on TV?" asked Mary Beth eagerly.

"Sure. If you can stand the show. Dreadful script. It'll air in July, they say."

"That's wonderful!!"

"It's not *Cyrano,*" he warned. "But thanks for the vote of confidence. I'll see you Monday, then." He was standing by his car.

There was a shadowed figure facing the wall not far from the Land Rover. Mary Beth realized suddenly that it was the drunk from across the street. He was urinating against the restaurant wall. Suddenly icy and weak, she reeled back a few steps and vomited onto the asphalt. She was aware, dimly, of Maggie and Nick catching her by the elbows as she began to fall, and of their voices somewhere far away, behind the shrieking Lords of Death.

"Mary Beth! Can we help?"

She couldn't answer.

"Do you think we should get her to a hospital, Maggie?"

"I think she flashed on something. Give her a minute. Can you get that guy to move on?" And when Nick was gone, "Mary Beth. Can you hear me?"

"I'll be okay," Mary Beth managed to say. She could hear better now, and the dim world was coming back into focus.

"Good. He's gone now," Maggie said. "Everything is okay."

"How are you doing?" Nick was back, gentle and worried.

"Better," said Mary Beth. Maggie was wiping her face carefully with a tissue.

"Hold her elbow a minute, Nick, okay?" Maggie took Mary Beth's bag and pulled out the keys to the Land Rover and opened the passenger door. Mary Beth was lifted carefully and put on the seat.

"Do you still feel sick?" Maggie asked, leaning in to stroke the blonde hair from her damp forehead.

"Not really. Just weak. Also disgusting."

"Don't worry. Put your head on your knees if you want. I'll drive." The door closed.

"Will she be all right?" Nick still sounded anxious.

"Sure. She's tough. She's just not very happy."

"Can I do anything else?"

"Not a thing. You're leaving her in the best of hands."

"That I know."

"Okay. We'll see you Monday."

"If she's all right."

"She'll not only be all right, she'll lead the way up the mountain. Listen, we'll bring the food."

"Okay, if I can bring the wine."

"Something to go with beef." She was climbing into the Land Rover.

"Right. Sure she'll be all right now?"

"I'll be fine," said Mary Beth sturdily.

The Land Rover moved out smoothly. As she slowed before leaving the parking lot, Maggie laid a gentle hand on Mary Beth's shoulder. "Okay now?" she asked.

"Yes. Just weak."

"Well, rest a little."

Mary Beth leaned back in the seat as they drove into the darkness, only dimly aware of something bulky in the back of the Land Rover. She dozed most of the way home. She woke once, and Maggie asked, "How are you doing?"

"Better."

"Mary Beth, sometimes you have to talk about things. Drag them out to look at them so you know just what it is you want to forget. Then you can start forgetting."

"I can't."

"It's like your story. It helps if you can name your enemy."

"Maggie, no. I'm afraid."

"Okay." Maggie sighed.

Mary Beth changed the subject. "Is there something in the back there?"

"Yes."

"What?"

"Secret. I'll show you tomorrow."

"You've got a hell of a lot of secrets, Maggie Ryan," complained Mary Beth drowsily.

"Don't we all."

"Well, Nick was a good one. I like him."

"Yeah. My favorite uncle."

Mary Beth dozed off again. She woke briefly once more before they reached home. Maggie was humming happily to herself.

X

7 Hunaapu
(June 15, 1968)

The mood was growing in him again. All the tension at work,
everybody always wanting something from him. May hadn't been
a bad month, nice weather, and she'd been nice too, in a good
mood. But last night she'd started pushing. Always wanting something from him. A guy had to be in control of his own life. Pa said,
"Stay in control, boy. There's ways to stay in control." But Pa had
been wrong. The cops coming in, blue shirts, big sexy guys. No!
No, maybe not big guys, just seemed that way when he'd been
thirteen. Probably just average guys. Sweaty smell of the blue
shirts. "Kid, where's your mother?" Watching Pa, handcuffs,
saying, "Listen, she was asking for it, you know? She was just
some whore!" The sweaty blue shirt again, "Where's your
mother, kid?" "She'll be home later." But they'd found out.
She'd been gone three years by then, she and her golden retriever.
And he'd had to go to the foster home. All rules and bean soup.
Old bitch running the place, running her husband, running him. He
took it a couple of years, ran away, got back in control. But now,
she was pushing again. Hassle at work, hassle at home. The mood
was growing.

But today was his Saturday off, so he had to bide his time. Better
to work from the job. No one kept very close tabs there, no time
clock to punch. Almost like being self-employed. Respectable. He
could bide his time. Next week sometime. He'd be working next
weekend. Or maybe sooner. Maybe even Monday.

The murderer turned to the classifieds. No puppies today, but there were kittens, as usual. Free to good homes. He could bide his time.

Saturday, Jane was a bit hung over. Word had come yesterday: the department had recommended her for tenure. Hal, too, had been recommended, and now they were both to be considered by the college committee. Jane's sense of dizzying relief that she had cleared this first hurdle was tempered a little by her sorrow for Linc. Cautiously, she had tried to comfort him; but his dark eyes were lifeless, and he taught his courses and cared for his finches like a big bearded automaton.

Roger's enthusiastic delight had known no bounds. He had bought champagne and they had celebrated with a giggly and juvenile night drinking it, watching old movies on TV, munching popcorn, and composing dirty limericks that had seemed hilarious at the time. Today, her head aching, she couldn't remember any.

Unfortunately, her work did not let up for hangovers. Summer school always proceeded at a killing pace, every day of the three-week session representing a week of classes in the regular school year. Even teaching a course she had taught before, it was hard work. Class did not meet on Saturdays, thank God, but the reading and grading went on. And on.

The *Verbal Learning Quarterly* had returned the galleys for her negation article too. Like most journals, the *VLQ* was very leisurely about publishing things it had accepted, but wanted immediate responses when it finally set something in type. So proofing the galleys was a high priority today.

She was stranded in her apartment. The idiot Volks was at the dealer again, suffering from catarrh or something. Ready Monday, they had cheerfully told her yesterday. So poor Roger, who could have dropped her by today on his way to Syracuse, would have to take time off Monday. Maybe she could find another ride.

This afternoon, too, she had invited Sergeant Rayburn from the Laconia police to come talk to the WAR meeting. They had shifted the meeting place to her apartment in honor of the Volks's indisposition. So, in addition to the two hours or so that the meeting would consume, she had to allow time to pick up the scattered newspapers and put clean towels in the bathroom and put the coffee on. Roger was helpful when she was so busy, but since he was spending the day in Syracuse and wouldn't be back till late, it was up to her.

She had read half of the exams by eleven o'clock, and put the stack down to get herself a cup of coffee. Sergeant Rayburn and the others should arrive by two. She could straighten the place, get a sandwich, and proof the galleys by then, and maybe start in on these boring exams again. She swooped up a bunch of books on infant behavior from her desk and stuck them on a shelf, then spread out the galleys and her manuscript on the desk and sat down with pencil and coffee to correct them. "Social Class Differences in the Acquisition of Negation." Jane Freemann, New York State University at Laconia. Couldn't even get her damn name right. She circled the final *n* and wrote in the symbol for deletion, then went on through the first paragraphs.

When the doorbell rang a few minutes before two, she had almost finished the proofreading. It was Maggie Ryan and Jackie Edwards, who had written that incredibly good paper on French kids. They were followed soon by three other members of the group, and then by Sergeant Rayburn. Eventually everyone arrived, and the sergeant gave a short talk and addressed himself to an array of questions.

"Why don't you have more rapists in jail?" asked Jane.

"Well, we try, of course. But besides all the usual problems of catching criminals, a lot of times the victims won't press charges."

"Why not?"

"I don't know. Reasons vary, I guess. Sometimes they say they want to at first and then later change their minds."

"Is it because they're afraid?" asked Jackie.

"Maybe. For some of them."

"But that would be true for any mugging," objected Monica. "Anyone could be afraid the guy would come back later for revenge."

"Well, it's true of rape especially."

"If they do press charges, do you usually get convictions?" asked Jane.

Sergeant Rayburn looked uncomfortable. "Sometimes. Other times it's pretty hard."

"Why?"

"It's usually just the victim's word against the accused's word."

Maggie said, "There's other evidence, too. Semen, hair, bruises."

"Yeah, bruises help."

"Does that mean the other evidence doesn't help?"

96

"Well, about half the time the guys are impotent. No semen. And there are a lot of false accusations. Grudges. So a defense lawyer can say the victim was willing. You know, led on his client. But bruises and cuts show she probably didn't really want it."

"So if you're raped but not beat up, you don't have a chance?"

"Not much of one."

"Because the defense will say you were willing!"

"Well, yes. Especially these days, if you've had a boyfriend or something. Or if you were wearing shorts or a miniskirt or something."

Terry said, "What about the rapist? What about his past record?"

"You generally can't bring that up in court. He's supposed to be judged just on the evidence of what he's accused of. Not his past life."

"But you just said the victim's past life could be brought up if it helped the defense. Along with her miniskirt."

"Well, that's the way it works."

"Look," said Maggie. "What if someone pulls a knife on me and demands my wallet and I give it to him. You catch him and bring him to court. And I testify that I gave him the wallet because he pulled a knife on me. As a general rule would you expect him to be convicted?"

"Yes, but of course it's hard to say, cases are so different."

"Just in general, I mean. In general, would the defense attorney cross-examine me and say, 'It's your fault because you led him on by wearing obviously expensive clothes, tempting the poor fellow'?"

Everyone smiled. Sergeant Rayburn said, "No."

"Would he say, 'Well, in the past you've been known to give money to your friends. So obviously you gave your wallet to this guy with a knife just because you're a generous person'?"

"No," admitted Sergeant Rayburn.

"But if it's sex the guy wants instead of money, suddenly it's my fault. I'm giving it away, or I'm wearing the wrong clothes."

Sergeant Rayburn shrugged. "That's just the way it is. That's how juries see it."

Maggie said, "I think you've answered Professor Freeman's question. About why more victims don't press charges."

There was a short silence. Sergeant Rayburn looked unhappy. "It's always hard for people who prosecute crimes," he proposed.

97

"Except that their morals aren't usually publicly attacked," said Jackie.

Sergeant Rayburn was increasingly uncomfortable.

"All right, sergeant," Jane said sympathetically, "it's not your fault that courts can be harder on rape victims than other victims. Maybe it would be useful if you told us what you need to make a good case."

"Okay." Sergeant Rayburn was pleased at the change of subject. "Let's say you've had several rapes or assaults in an area."

"Like the Triangle Murderer," suggested Terry.

"Yeah. That's a good example. Pretty extreme, because there most of the victims are dead."

Monica said, "At least they don't have to face the defense attorney."

"Yeah. Well. We do have a little information from people who were driving by the area at the time of the murders. Since it's on the highway, they all mention cars. A lot of them mention a gray or a blue Chevy, sixty-four or sixty-five. So we're looking for that kind of car. We check the victims for evidence, of course, but there isn't much. A few hairs, Caucasian, and a shirt button—common type, comes on J.C. Penney's shirts. The old lady was holding that. No special pattern among the victims, except they were all alone in their cars. And that's about it."

"Really? That's all? No more clues?"

Rayburn shrugged. "Who knows? They've combed the areas. And there's a fine collection of things that might be clues, or might not. Out of seven victims, there were beer cans near five, two of them Bud. Is that a clue? Two discarded magazines. Tissues near three. A yogurt pot, half a dozen cigarette stubs, a kitten killed by a car, a pair of sunglasses, fast-food wrappers, old plastic bags, sales receipts, a white terry tube sock. You name it. Maybe some of them are clues. Maybe not. There's no pattern."

"Seven women dead, and no pattern!"

"I can advise you to stay in your cars around Syracuse. Be on guard. Don't do anyone any favors. He's using some trick, something a lot of women would fall for."

"Or men," said Terry.

"Maybe. I'm just trying to explain how things are."

"Okay," said Maggie. "Suppose I'm lucky enough to come out alive. What evidence would you guys like to have?"

"Identification, first. Anything you can get. License number, description. If there's a witness to any of it, get that name too. Don't wash. If you go to the hospital first, explain that it was rape so they'll get samples and photos. And call us right away."

"Got it," said Maggie.

"If you can mark him somehow it would help. Scratch him or something."

"If he's armed?"

"Yeah, right, don't fight guns or knives. That's dumb, usually. But look for identifying marks. Or take things if you can, his comb or a paper. Or if he gets you in his car, hide something of yours under the seat."

"And then be ready to prosecute if you can bear it," said Jane briskly. "Look, it's about time we let Sergeant Rayburn go. We've learned a lot, I think."

There was a chorus of agreement, and thanks.

Sergeant Rayburn grinned. "Guess I learned a couple of things too," he said.

"'Well, thank you," said Jane. "Maggie, Monica, can you help me bring in the coffee?"

Most of the group stood up to stretch and to gather around Sergeant Rayburn as Jane and her two helpers went to the kitchen to bring back coffee and cups and cookies. Jane set her tray down on the coffee table. A good session, she thought, as she played hostess and poured out the coffee; unpleasant in some ways, of course, but realism was what they wanted.

She glanced around the room. Most of the women were subdued and thoughtful, like Jackie Edwards standing frowning at the desk, sipping the mug of coffee that Maggie had handed her, or Monica quietly passing the plate of cookies. Terry and three others now talking to Sergeant Rayburn were laughing a little, though, at some joke he had made. What should the group do next? Maybe it was time to talk to a lawyer. She'd ask Roger if there were any attorneys who might speak to the group.

Her head was a little better. After everyone left, she finished tidying up, then went back to her desk to finish her proofreading. Staring down at the neatly printed long pages with her own scribbled marks, she suddenly felt a wave of hopelessness. The whole last ten years seemed lost, a mistake, all that work to get her degree, to publish, to impress her colleagues. Silly to think she'd ever get tenure. The departmental approval that she and Roger had celebrated so giddily last night was just one step. There were just too

99

many obstacles. But she sat down and turned her mind sternly to proofing the last few paragraphs, and then she graded some more exams. By the time Roger returned late that afternoon she was ready to launch herself into the struggle again.

Sue came back to Walton Street from a day as escort to the visiting Russians at about four o'clock, and she grilled Jackie and Maggie thoroughly about the WAR meeting she had had to miss. Mary Beth remained in the living room trying to read, but noticed that Jackie seemed morose and quiet about it, and that it was chiefly Maggie, clanking pots and pans as she fixed dinner, who answered most of Sue's questions. Sue was fascinated by the bits of information they had received about the Triangle Murderer.

"We should get up a posse or something," she declared.

"Innocent until proven guilty," Maggie reminded her. "They can't arrest everyone with a gray or blue Chevy and a J.C. Penney shirt."

"Pooh. In this case I'm all for a police state."

Maggie asked, "Frank's coming tonight, isn't he, Jackie?"

"Right."

"Oh God," said Sue. "Guess I'll get into my shabbies so I won't steal him away from you, gorgeous creature that I am. I don't think he could take a third one of us." Her high heels went clicking up the stairs.

"You okay, Jackie?" Maggie's voice asked.

"Yeah."

"Something on your mind?"

"Yeah. I'll tell you about it later. I have to talk to someone first."

"Sure. Do you know if Frank likes Provençal cooking?"

"He says the only thing he hates is bean soup."

"Well, then, we're home free."

Mary Beth took a deep breath and went to freshen herself up before dinner. In the mirror she looked pretty good, she thought, blonde hair shining again, the blue eyes and firm mouth suggesting the confidence that wasn't really there. Maybe she was getting better. But she knew too well that there was still damage inside, waiting to surface unexpectedly again, when she saw a chipmunk or a drunk by a wall. Ros said you can't erase time.

But she couldn't think about it, couldn't talk about it. Surely Maggie was wrong, talking wouldn't help. Surely it was fading by

100

now, would all disappear in time. Time heals, Nick had said. Already, most of the time, she didn't think about it. And surely she could get the thesis out of the way and get back to Guatemala soon.

If only she could feel that she had done the right thing.

Forget it, don't think about it. She dabbed on more cologne to block the ugly smell.

Dinner was fairly cheerful. Frank was teasing Jackie about a report she had made on Victor Hugo, which she defended with spirit and good humor, and Maggie's beef stew was especially good, as her dinners often were on Saturdays when she had time to do things the French way. About halfway through dinner, there was the blare of loud music from across the street.

"Heck," said Sue. "Is it my turn?"

"I'll come with you," said Maggie. The two of them disappeared and presently the volume was lowered a little. They came back a minute later, Sue looking glum but Maggie unaccountably cheerful.

"Bad news," said Sue. "Looks like party night."

"Gross," said Jackie. "Let's get out of here, Frank."

"Done. We'll go to the flicks." He patted Jackie's shoulder possessively. "Listen, that was a great stew or whatever it was, Maggie."

"Daube. Thanks."

"Haven't eaten like that since Paris. And not often there, because I was too poor."

"No one's ever rich enough for Paris."

"Well, that's true too."

"Here. Have some macédoine before you run off."

Mary Beth took some too. She hadn't had much appetite for months, but it was important to show Maggie that she appreciated the effort that had gone into it. They had coffee, and then Frank and Jackie left. Mary Beth started clearing up the kitchen.

"You made a lot of daube tonight," she observed. "It was good. We'll have another whole meal from it, won't we?"

"Yep," agreed Maggie. "Monday lunch."

"Aha. I see now. Frank is an accidental beneficiary. You're not trying for his heart through his stomach."

"God, no. It's for the picnic. I just thought we could take the camp stove up with us and warm up the daube. It's better the second day. And Nick will have something good to drink with it. He knows about food."

101

"Are you sure you want me along, Maggie?"

"You mean you'd be bored if we started talking about old times?"

"No. I'd be fascinated," admitted Mary Beth.

"Well, nosy, come along. And you too, Sue."

"Sorry," said Sue. "Much as I'd love to meet this talented uncle of yours, the first problem is to survive this three-week summer session. Those visiting dignitaries didn't help. I'm going up to work now."

"I'm going up too," said Maggie. "I've got a big project due Wednesday. See you later, scullery maid." She and Sue went upstairs.

Mary Beth finished the dishes and scrubbed the kitchen, always a big job when Maggie's French muse hit her. Afterward she went upstairs herself to work on Ixil verbs again. It was slowing down the thesis considerably, a fascinating but time-consuming problem. She had brought home a stack of books on other Mayan languages earlier in the week, and was working her way through them in the hopes of finding a historical explanation that would satisfy Professor Greene.

After half an hour, the music across the street rose in volume again. Even in Mary Beth's room, at the back of the house, she could hear the words distinctly. It was the Beatles' "All You Need Is Love." Not good study music. She cursed to herself and started to close the window tighter, wondering how Maggie could stand it. But she paused with her hand on the sash.

Somewhere another sound had begun.

Richard Wagner. *Tristan und Isolde.*

Birgit Nilsson's enormous soprano voice.

It filled the night. It was huge and sonorous. Mary Beth frowned to herself and went down to the front porch. Sue was already there, looking up in disbelief.

"It's coming from Maggie's goddamn room," she said.

It was true. The gargantuan voice, high and powerful, was rolling from the upstairs window of their own house.

Across the street at the party, several dismayed people had come out the open front door. Someone pointed up at Maggie's window. All up and down the street, in fact, people were coming out to hear what was happening. They watched the two houses and grinned or covered their ears. In a minute the Beatles went up in volume a notch or two.

102

Birgit Nilsson rose to the occasion. With Wagner's amplified orchestration booming beneath her, the powerful soprano voice, swollen now to a shrillness beyond bearing, soared ever more piercingly through the night. The music from across the street sounded thin in the occasional rests of Wagner's thundering music.

A couple of ear-splitting minutes went by. The Rolling Stones took over from the Beatles. Nilsson started the same aria again and repeated her triumph. Mary Beth laughed in spite of herself, and Sue was crowing with delight, bouncing up and down with her hands clapped over her ears.

The music from across the street suddenly abated, and someone emerged and started toward them waving a broom with a white handkerchief tied to the handle.

Birgit Nilsson lowered her voice abruptly.

"Truce?" yelled the boy with the white flag. It was Bill, Mary Beth saw.

"Anything you say, Bill." Maggie was leaning out her window, elbows on the sill.

"What do you want?"

"I want to hear my own music."

"That's what we want too."

"Right."

"But, um, we're having a party."

"I'm not. I'm just listening to records. I just want to hear my own music."

"Oh."

"Right."

"How about if we close the doors and windows?"

"Fine with me."

"Will you close yours?"

"Not on a nice night like this. Why should I?"

"Because . . . heck."

"I just want to hear my own music."

"You've got a new stereo outfit, huh."

"Yep. Good one."

"Yeah. Listen, if you can't hear ours will you keep it a little lower?"

"Sure. I don't want to bother anybody. I just want to hear my own music."

"Okay. We'll see if this works."

He disappeared into the house again, and the front doors and windows closed. They caught a glimpse of Todd's angry glowering face before the door shut. In a minute Mary Beth, her jangled ears listening very hard, heard the faint throb of the party records again; and then, high and sweet and very soft in the June air, music from Maggie's room. Birgit Nilsson?

No. Maggie had switched to the Beatles too.

Down the street a little knot of neighbors applauded and cheered into the near-silence. Sue joined in, and others up and down the street. Mary Beth felt exhilarated. She rushed into the house, well ahead of Sue, and met Maggie coming down the stairs. She threw her arms around her.

"That was the most wonderful thing ever!" she cried.

Maggie, pleased, grinned back. "Hardly that," she said. "But thanks."

"How did you . . . oh Jeez!" Several things suddenly fell into place.

"I told you I'd show you today."

"But my God, Maggie, what if they catch you?"

"Catch her what?" asked Sue, arriving at last.

"She stole those speakers from the theatre last night!"

"Stole, nothing. They needed fixing," Maggie objected.

"My God," said Sue, pleased and appalled.

"Besides," said Maggie, "they'll be back in the theatre safe and sound on Monday. Better than when they left."

"Jeez," said Mary Beth, shaking her head.

Maggie looked at her owlishly. "Some problems require drastic measures. Don't you think so?"

Mary Beth considered, and grinned. "I think it was the most wonderful thing ever!"

Upstairs, the Beatles sang "A Little Help from My Friends."

XI

9 Iiq
(June 17, 1968)

She was dead now, no more threat. The murderer pushed aside the long dark hair and, very carefully, cut the triangle into the young cheek. Done. Now, walk to the car calmly, get in. Back to the highway, driving coolly, back in control again.

The Christian conquerors teach that days don't begin until midnight. The Maya know that it takes longer to hand over the burdens of time, and that the influence of the incoming god may begin at sunset. The day known as Monday, June 17, to those who count by the Gregorian calendar was pleasantly breezy, as befitted the Ixil 9 Iiq; but shortly after sunset it became one of the most tragic of Mary Beth's life. A Mayan traditionalist might have attributed the change to the coming of that doubly unlucky day, 10 Aqbal. Ten, the number of death, of violence. Aqbal, the day of evil in men's hearts; the day of Night.

But it had all begun quite cheerfully.

Maggie had packed the speakers and amplifier carefully into the Land Rover. Jackie's brake repairs were not yet finished, so she needed to borrow Maggie's rusty Ford another day. Besides, the Land Rover was roomier for transporting speakers. Maggie had borrowed Sue's backpack in case Nick needed one, and had packed her own and Mary Beth's with the camp stove and the food. She hummed lightheartedly as she worked.

"You're happy to see him, aren't you?" Mary Beth had said, tightening the top of the salad dressing jar.

"Yes, but that's only part of it," Maggie had confessed. "It's just good to know that's behind me. It was a very bad time, and Nick was there. But I can see him now and just enjoy the friendship. The bad memories are there, way in the background, but the good ones are too. It doesn't hurt anymore. It hurt quite a lot for a while."

"Your cliché love affair," said Mary Beth daringly.

Maggie nodded calmly. "His name was Rob. A professional actor, like Nick. Gloriously bright and handsome. I fell in love, and even agreed to marry him. He was fun. And then I found out that he was already committed to someone else."

"I see."

"Well, I told you it was cliché."

"Rob played violin."

Maggie gave her a reproachful look. "Why do you bother to ask when you know all about it already?"

Mary Beth started packing the forks and spoons and said, "Nick told me his wife died."

"Yes. It was a very bad time. But he seems okay now too."

"So you're free now." Mary Beth, despite herself, felt envious. "No wonder you're so happy."

"Free. No, not really," said Maggie thoughtfully. "It'll always be with me. I've learned from it, and I'll never make that mistake again. But I'm back in control, you see. If I can see Uncle Nick like a normal human being, I can do anything."

"You're brave, Maggie."

"Brave, nothing!" Maggie's eyes met hers, merrily. "I've got this sadistic friend Mary Beth who keeps forcing me to do things and go places when I don't want to."

"Maggie, I'm sorry. I didn't know."

"Don't sell yourself short, Mary Beth. Your cruel demands come from a very intelligent subconscious. It's been right every time."

"Thanks, I guess."

"Wish I could do something for you. Anyway, let's get this stuff into the Land Rover."

The day was another fine one, the sky streaked with a few clouds but basically sunny and smelling of clover and mock orange. Sue and Jackie saw them off, professing to be jealous but adamantly refusing all invitations to come along.

"Thanks, but I've got a date at the library this afternoon," Jackie explained.

"I'm too busy too," Sue said. "Besides, you won't catch me in the same vehicle with stolen property. You're going to need me to stand bail."

They drove the twenty miles happily, most of it on superhighway. After they exited, the last three miles were along a winding country road. They pulled into the parking lot a few minutes early to find Nick already there and out of his car, studying a map of the park on a signboard. They didn't need Sue's backpack after all: he was wearing one already.

"Great place," he said as they came up. "Looks like we can get to the top of that ridge back there, right?"

"It takes some climbing," said Mary Beth. "But there's a good trail all the way."

"Have you been up there too?" he asked Maggie.

"Not yet. Not to that part. But you can believe Mary Beth. She's an expert mountaineer."

"I know." He grinned at her. "Anyone who can climb the Cuchu-whatchamacallits is expert enough for me."

"Cuchumatanes," said Mary Beth.

"Well, let's go then."

They started up the trail and Mary Beth noticed again how accurate and smooth his movements were for a big man—not the shambling heavy walk of a bear but the liquid tread of a leopard or lion, muscular and precise. There were ferns and maples here on the north side of the ridge, and slate outcroppings. After they had walked along a hundred yards or so the path suddenly became steeper. There was broken stone in the cliff side. They passed a sign that read, "Danger, Fallen Rocks. Do Not Leave Trail."

Nick said conversationally, "You know, when I was a kid, a sign like that was not a prohibition. It was a challenge."

Maggie's blue eyes flicked to his, delighted, and then she bounded up the cliff side, scrambling nimbly among the rocks and branches to gain a foothold up higher. Nick was right behind her. They disappeared behind some rocks farther up. Mary Beth, uncertain, waited a second and then continued around the next bend to find them sitting above her on a big rock that almost overhung the trail.

"Want to come with us?" asked Maggie. "The direct route?"

"No, thanks," said Mary Beth, smiling up at them. "I'm just a

107

simple cross-country runner. Not a mountain goat. I'll just meet you at the top."

"Okay. We'll see you up there. Right where this trail intersects the one along the top of the ridge."

"Fine. Give a hoot if you get into trouble."

"Okay."

"I can tell the theatre to get the understudy ready."

"Won't do any good," said Nick, smiling. "They'll carry me on in a basket. The show must go on and all that. Anyway, there's no show tonight. My bones have till tomorrow night to mend."

"See you in a few minutes, then."

She watched them a moment as they started up the cliff, two well-trained athletes, and reflected that an actor would have to keep in very good shape to perform the strenuous three-hour role of Cyrano. Then she moved on up the trail, running from time to time for the pleasure of it, but not working too hard out of regard for the food in her backpack. The freshness of the day and the friendly solitude of the woods almost made her forget her own worthlessness. It was a good day—Iiq, the day of Wind.

Tomorrow was the bad one.

Nearing the top, she slowed a little; the trail, she saw, would double back once more and then reach the top of the ridge. She caught a glimpse of them through the trees above her and paused, surprised. They had shed their backpacks and were sitting together on a big sunny rock, Maggie bent over, face in her hands, weeping. Mary Beth was astonished. She had never seen her proud, determined friend cry. Well, Maggie, not as tough as you pretend to be. Nick, quiet and sympathetic beside her, was patting her on the shoulder. Mary Beth suddenly felt jealous, but then she didn't know why. Jealous of Nick for being in Maggie's confidence? Jealous of Maggie for being able to tell? No, of course not. She went on around the turn in the trail, kicking stones noisily, and decided that in any case it had nothing to do with her. She was on her own, a worthless and used-up creature who had no right to expect any interest from anyone. But then why did Maggie stand by her? And claim to be grateful?

Ros had said women need to be strong, it is difficult to endure. The hardest lesson is to learn to bear things.

By the time she reached the top of the trail she'd mastered her unhappiness again, and she was ready to look at the amazing view from the ridge. On one side Litchfield Gorge dropped abruptly, the small river at the bottom shining thin amid the foliage. The slope of the other side, the one they had just finished climbing, was not so steep, but it still fell a long way before merging into the surrounding hills. The sky, paled by thin streaky clouds, bent cheerfully over all.

Maggie had spread a big plaid blanket on the grass, and as Mary Beth came up to her she smiled, sunny and serene as the day itself, no trace of tears. Refreshed even. "You must have run," she said, reaching for Mary Beth's backpack.

"It's that kind of day," said Mary Beth, handing it to her. "Makes you want to do things. Like run or climb up cliffs."

"Right. It's wonderful." Maggie was setting up the camp stove and putting the pot of beef daube on it to warm. There was salad and crusty French bread. Nick had brought a good Beaujolais and even some wineglasses, wrapped carefully for the hike. Mary Beth left Maggie to arrange things and walked over to the point of the ridge. Nick was sitting there, back against a tree, looking out at the incredible landscape. The rounded hills, cut by gorges, were leafy in the first maturity of summer. The benevolent sky was reflected from the thread of water far below. On the other side she could see the edge of the parking lot below, the Land Rover and Nick's car recognizable on it, and even farther away the tiny shapes of cars on the superhighway. There were parking lots and a few buildings, small and white, near the highway exit, but everything else was nature.

"It's lovely," she said to Nick as she settled under a tree a few yards from his.

"Mm-hmm." He welcomed her with a friendly smile.

They sat for a few minutes in comfortable silence, and then he began to sing quietly, contentedly, "Summer is Icumen In." His voice was pleasant, trained. In a moment, a second, lighter voice joined his; they turned their heads to see that Maggie too had found a tree nearby to lean against. She and Nick looked at each other seriously as they sang the ancient canon, their voices meshing well. Mary Beth couldn't remember the words but came in on the "cuccu's." When they had finished Maggie smiled and looked out over the landscape again, and all three sat quietly for a moment, feeling at one with the breeze and the sunshine. The insects droned and the hawks soared, and far below a little blue car pulled off the highway ramp and parked in the shade of the trees. Maggie stood up and stretched.

"Should be ready by now," she said. "Anyone else hungry?"

"Ravenous," said Nick.

They went back to the spread blanket. Maggie was right; as far as Mary Beth could tell, the daube was better this time around, and the wine good. She wished she had more appetite, Maggie and Nick were enjoying it so much. They were undisturbed except for one family with two young boys that came puffing up the trail, exclaimed at the view for a few minutes, and then departed immediately down the trail again.

Nick took another helping of daube and said, "I haven't enjoyed anything this much for ages, Maggie. A very good idea to come here."

"Yeah, I was ready for it too." She looked at him thoughtfully and added, "It must have been a bad year."

"Yeah." He looked down at his plate. "You remember how crazy I was at the beginning. You helped me out of that. Blaming her for dying, for going away. Or blaming myself. If only I had been there, if only I had done this or that . . . You helped me then, Maggie."

Maggie shrugged silently.

"And your heart plays tricks on you," he continued. "You start seeing yourself as the victim."

"Well, sure, you're hurt too."

"Yes, but you get the illusion it was all aimed at you. I mean, the center of the universe is Nick O'Connor, that's obvious, isn't it? So I was sure there was some bigger cosmic plan, somehow aimed at me. It was all for a purpose. There must be justice somewhere. Fate is fair after all, and for a while I expected every role I got, every woman I met, to be a wonderful surprise. And of course I was always disappointed."

"Yeah, that's not very realistic," said Maggie.

He smiled at her. "It was just so unfair to have Lisette taken away, there must be something to balance it, I thought. It was too frightening to imagine an unjust universe where I could be a victim without cause."

Mary Beth sat almost without breathing. He was speaking directly to her, it seemed.

"But eventually it became clear that there wasn't going to be any cosmic balancing act. No compensation for me. And that's when the depression really set in, the feeling that I wasn't worth anything after all. And guilt too."

110

That's how it is, thought Mary Beth, he's right. And she saw that Maggie too was intent on his words, the blue eyes shadowed with her own pain and with his.

"How did you get through?" asked Maggie. "Work?"

"Yes." He nodded. "George helped. Bullied me through. Just the way you did earlier." He smiled at her and went on. "George was wonderful. You see, I could hardly think of the future at all—it was so terrible to think of so many days still to come. But he kept prodding me—do this, do that—and it was easier to do it than fight him. He kept my minutes filled. And finally, a few weeks ago, I came out of it."

"You came out of it?" asked Mary Beth. Her voice was husky.

"The worst of it. I can enjoy things again. Look forward to things. Sleep for whole nights. I'll always miss her. It will always seem terribly unfair. But it isn't crippling anymore."

"You're free again," said Mary Beth.

"Free. Not really," he said, echoing Maggie's words, and then quoted, "I cannot but remember such things were, that were most precious to me."

"I see."

"I don't know if I'd want to be free, if that means I wouldn't care anymore. But Lisette's death doesn't control my life anymore. And, yes, I'm free to enjoy a sunny day and a splendid view and friends."

Maggie reached over and patted his big hand. "I'm glad," she said.

Mary Beth blinked down at her plate, not seeing it. She was amazed, because he—he, that glorious Cyrano, that jovial uncle—had felt worthless too, and he hadn't been able to understand such an unjust world.

Now he could. Now he could even tell her about it.

She was not the only one.

She looked up to find the dark clear eyes on her. "I hope all this confession didn't upset you," said Nick uneasily. He didn't know her very well, she remembered with surprise.

"No," she said.

But Maggie, who did know her, said, "She means yes. Yes, but in a good way."

"Thank you," said Mary Beth to him gratefully.

He was pleased. "Thank you for listening."

Maggie shoved a bowl of fresh strawberries in front of them. "Okay. Enough profundity," she said briskly.

"Right!" Nick beamed at her. "Report time. Uncle wants to know. What was the diagnosis? Was your project a success?"

"In every way," said Maggie. "It was just a short in the jack." Between strawberries, she told him of Birgit Nilsson's shrill and stirring victory. Mary Beth chimed in with details, and Nick enjoyed it all hugely.

"With thy grim looks and the thunderlike percussion of your sounds," he intoned, "thou mad'st thine enemies shake."

Maggie grinned. "I didn't look grim at all. But the rest is accurate enough."

As they cleared up the picnic, Nick said, "You mentioned that you were taking some self-defense lessons."

"Only a few. But listen!" Maggie looked at him, sparkling. "Why don't you play the villain a few minutes, Unk? So far I've only practiced with other women. Okay?"

"Sure," he agreed. "Nick the Ripper at your service." They moved to the widest spot of the ridge. Mary Beth, kneeling to fold the blanket, watched, amused.

"Okay," Maggie said. "Grab me a few times."

He reached for her wrist; she karate-chopped his arm away before he touched her. He started to kick her; she deflected his leg, shifting the force to the side. He lunged for her throat; she smashed his hands away.

"What do you think?" she asked eagerly.

"Not bad. You're quick and strong." He picked up her wrist and examined her hand. "Good grip. And you don't pull punches. Most women do. You're all set when you know someone is about to attack you. But before you replace Bruce Lee, show me what you do when you don't know."

"What do you mean?"

He grinned, lifted the wrist that he was still holding. "Suppose someone cons you and you don't know his intentions until you've already been grabbed?"

Her eyes narrowed. She stared an instant at his hand clamped on her arm, and then chopped down on his forearm with her other hand, and whipped up her knee to hit it too.

"Ouch," said Nick calmly, his grip unrelenting.

She struggled back. "Damnit, you sneak!" She kicked at his

groin but he turned his hip into the kick, grabbed her ankle with his free hand, and lifted. Off balance, she could not stay upright.

He lowered her to the ground and let go. "That's the way it'll be, Maggie," he said seriously. "You may not see it coming."

"So what the hell do I do?"

"You're halfway there already. Fit and willing to go for blood. That's good."

"Yeah, tell me that sometime when I'm not flat on my back."

"I'm not kidding. I'm stronger than you are, but strength isn't as important as knowing where to apply it. Here, hold my wrist." She scrambled up and grasped it with determination. He said, "Okay. I try to get away like this . . ." He jerked down. "No good. You've still got me. Like this . . ." His arm jerked up and out of her grip. "I escape."

"But that's just because my thumb slipped . . . Oh, I see."

"Right. The power all goes against the weakest point. If my thumb is on top and four fingers under, jerk up. If my fingers are on top, jerk down against my lonely thumb. Divided we fall. That's lesson one."

"Okay."

"And use every muscle you've got against the weak spot."

She offered him her arm again, and he took it, thumb on top. Her knees flexed a little and then jerked straight as she uncoiled and snapped her arm up and back, breaking his grip. She beamed—but only for an instant, because he had stepped forward at the height of her move and pushed her unbalanced body back. She landed on her back and he lunged after her, pinning her arms. Mary Beth averted her eyes, fearful that the screaming in her mind would start.

"Don't tell me," said Maggie's voice a little shakily. "Lesson two?"

"Right."

"But I really did break your grip."

"*Yes*, Mademoiselle. You really did."

"And then you smashed me anyway."

"Gosh, I'm such a cad."

"Because I thought that breaking the grip was the end of the episode. But in real life it won't be." Mary Beth peeked back at them; they were both sitting quietly on the grass, Maggie frowning as she continued. "In real life he'll keep coming at me, so I'll have to keep going at him."

113

"Yeah. Lesson two is that a fight isn't a set of isolated punches. They flow together."

"Like a gymnastics routine."

"Right. Plan your moves so you aren't off balance, you're ready to follow up your success with a surprise counterattack against his vulnerable areas. His eyes, the underside of his nose, the hollow of his throat."

"His balls."

"Only if he's distracted. Because most of us fellas, even the cads, know we're vulnerable there, and protecting ourselves is second nature. We've been practicing all our lives. You can try a feint to the eyes or the throat first to distract him, then grab. But don't stand back and kick. You can be flipped back off balance."

"Yeah, I know, you just demonstrated." Maggie looked at him resentfully. "Where did my sweet, pacific Uncle Nick learn all these dirty tricks?"

"Contact sports. Army. Stage combat lessons. Working as bouncer in a bar."

"All the things women aren't supposed to do. Because we might get hurt."

"Yep."

"All right, then." Maggie bounced to her feet resolutely. "Private Ryan reporting to Parris Island, 'sarge. What's lesson three?"

For thirty minutes Mary Beth watched them. Once Maggie invited her to join in, but she preferred to look on. Nick's advice was simple: break the attacker's grip, follow up instantly to hurt him, and escape to a safer place as soon as possible. Putting the advice into practice was harder. He showed her a number of basic counter-moves and counterattacks. Maggie was an apt pupil, already quick and athletic. Soon she managed to lever Nick away from her arm or throat, even throw him several times. Finally she plunked herself down on the grass next to Mary Beth, pleased and tired.

"That was better than hours of Ed Hamlin, Unk," she said. "But you didn't say anything about weapons."

"If he's got one, it's a problem. Focus on it. Obey him, soothe him, get control of it if you safely can." He grinned. "On the other hand, if you've got a weapon—a baseball bat, a ring of keys, whatever—wham him quick."

Nick glanced at his watch and suddenly looked alarmed. "God, Maggie, the *Ernest in Love* people will be starting rehearsals in an hour. We've got to get those speakers back!"

114

They finished packing hastily and hurried down the trail. On the way they decided that they would put the sound system into Nick's car and he and Maggie would return it. Mary Beth objected at first; she could take it to the theatre and take Maggie home afterward, and save Nick the round trip. But he shook his head. "Look, Mary Beth, it's my day off. I'm enjoying it, and I'm going to hang around as long as you two let me. So if you take her back to Laconia, you'll find me driving right behind you."

"Okay." She smiled at him. "Heaven knows I've got work to do." He had said that work had pulled him through too.

The big speakers, however, clearly wouldn't fit into Nick's car, and they finally decided to leave the sound system in the Land Rover and trade cars. Mary Beth would drive Nick's back to Laconia; Nick and Maggie would use the Land Rover to return the speakers and then drive to Laconia, where Nick would eventually retrieve his own car.

In fact, Mary Beth found that she needed the solitude that the drive home provided, to reflect on what Nick had said and what it might mean to her. There was something in Nick's story that had to do with Tip. But at that point her mind veered away again.

When she got back Jackie still had Maggie's car out, so she parked carefully to leave room for it. She went in to find clouds of smoke and Sue cursing in several languages. Jackie took over dinner duty today from Maggie and had put in a cake to bake before running off to some appointment. Sue had just been roused from her labors upstairs by the smell of burning, and was trying now to air out the kitchen.

"Irresponsible," fumed Sue. "This younger generation."

"Same generation as you," said Mary Beth. She inspected the chunk of charcoal in the cake pan and decided the kitchen would recover faster if the charred remains were taken outside. She placed it near the back fence and then came in to open all the doors and windows that weren't open already. The smoke receded slowly, and she and Sue got back to work. Mary Beth was finding that some of the other Mayan languages had verb systems very similar to Ixil's, but the overall pattern was not yet clear to her. From time to time she paused to think gratefully of what Nick had said. She thought, I'll tell Maggie, maybe; and for the first time did not dismiss the thought instantly in fear.

Frank called for Jackie. Sue told him she was at the library, and

115

hung up grumbling. "First Peter, now Frank. Wish Jackie would take care of her own boyfriends."

At six-thirty Sue was no longer angry, just weary and abused. She stuck her head in Mary Beth's door to say she'd given up waiting for dinner and was off to Misha's early to cadge some food. "To each according to her need," she declaimed, and left carrying enough books to show that she wouldn't be back for a while. Mary Beth, surprised at how late it was, went downstairs and dutifully ate some cheese and a banana, and made some coffee, Ixil style. That at least she could still taste.

Around seven Nick and Maggie arrived, laughing and warm. "Hi, Mary Beth. Dinner's over, huh?" Maggie asked, dropping her backpack on the floor.

"Well, actually, Jackie seems to have forgotten that it's her turn. So we haven't had much. Sue went to eat with Misha."

"Yeah, I saw my car was still gone. Where is Jackie?"

"I don't know for sure. Sue said she went to campus early this afternoon. She's probably at the library; she said something about that."

"Well, we're all entitled to a mistake occasionally. Listen, Nick, let me run this stuff upstairs and I'll take you to the Steamboat. Do you like Victorian?"

"Houses, yes. Food, no."

"Well, you're in luck. Food is plain American, not too awful, with pseudo-Victorian names. Omelette à la Bernhardt."

"With ham."

She grinned. "No translations needed, I see. Back in a minute." She sailed up the stairs, trailing backpacks and plaid blankets.

"Here's your car key," said Nick to Mary Beth.

"Thanks. Here's yours."

"Someplace I could wash my hands?" he asked.

"Sure. The bathroom's upstairs. Or here in the kitchen?"

"Kitchen's fine."

"Any problems getting those speakers back?"

"Well, the stage manager for *Ernest in Love* arrived early for his rehearsal. I had to head him off in the parking lot and spin yarns about stage managing in New York while Maggie got the last bits in and hooked up." He was scrubbing his burly arms up as far as the elbows.

"Spin yarns?" she repeated.

"About how professional actors are saved time and again by no-

116

ble and quick-thinking stage managers.'' He gave her a droll look as he dried off.

"At least you didn't have to tell him different ways to get to the moon, like Cyrano.''

He laughed. "Maggie said that too. It's true, after today I'll be able to do that scene with a lot of conviction.''

He seemed such a cheerful man, it was hard to believe what he'd been through. Mary Beth was heartened. He wet a paper towel and wiped his face and balding head.

"Do you want to sit down awhile?''

"Oh, I'm fine. Maggie's a rather exhausting friend to have, that's all.''

"She is that.''

"Nonsense!'' Maggie gusted into the kitchen, black curls brushed. She had changed to a fresh shirt, bright red. "Listen, let's go. *Je meurs de faim.*''

"She's always hungry too. Have you noticed?'' Nick asked Mary Beth.

"Yes, I have.'' She grinned at Maggie. "A living reproach to the satisfied.''

"Why don't you quit analyzing my unfortunate metabolic rate and come with us, Mary Beth?''

"No, really, I've eaten. And I've found some interesting stuff for my thesis. I want to keep working at it.''

"Work! God! I'm getting so far behind! But I have to eat,'' Maggie added hastily.

"You can always stay up late to work.''

"Right. Sleep I can skip, not food. Come on, uncle, before famine strikes us down.'' She grabbed a piece of dry bread and popped it in her mouth on the way to the door.

Nick grinned and shrugged at Mary Beth, and followed her out. Mary Beth looked after them fondly. She had friends, she had work, and the rest might someday be okay. It was okay now for Nick. She went upstairs again to work on her thesis.

The sun set.

It was a little after ten and she was still working hard when the officer arrived, and Mary Beth heard what he had to say and covered her face with her hands. She made a huge effort and said, "I can't. But my friend—let me get my friend.''

"Your friend?''

"At the Steamboat. Please." She was holding herself together with strands of pure will.

He drove her there in the patrol car and followed her in. Little bits of reality, like snapshots, clicked into her consciousness. The smell of cigarette smoke. A big placard inside the door proclaiming "Nostalgia Night, Starring Fats Waller." She stepped past the line of booths, lined with fancy white gingerbread woodwork, and looked around the crowded room. "Ain't She Sweet" was just coming to an end, fast and cheerful, and the dance floor was jammed with people. Mary Beth looked around frantically. Where was she?

"Where is she?" the officer asked. Officer Morton, he had said.

Then she saw them, across the floor. Maggie in her red shirt, dancing joyfully, and big Nick matching her stride for agile stride three feet away, two supple happy people moving harmoniously in the light of the Victorian lamps. "There," said Mary Beth, and started around the dance floor.

The music changed—the tempo was slow now. Maggie started off the floor, but Nick caught her hand and smiled and shook his head. Humoring him, she let him draw her close and he swirled her around a few steps, Fred and Ginger, as Mary Beth worked her way through the crowd toward them. The officer followed her discreetly.

Mary Beth did not hesitate; she tapped Nick urgently on the arm. He looked around slowly, like someone waking up. Maggie pulled back from Nick's arms in confusion, and for a second stared at him in complete lost panic. Then she saw Mary Beth.

"What is it?" She reached for Mary Beth's hand. "Something's terribly wrong."

"It's Jackie."

Maggie's quick blue eyes noted Officer Morton's presence, then returned to Mary Beth. "What about Jackie?" she asked gently.

"They think she's dead, Maggie," whispered Mary Beth with the last shreds of her control. "With a triangle on her cheek."

XII

10 Aqbal
(June 18, 1968)

The rest of the night was a blur to Mary Beth. They all went with Officer Morton to someplace official, the medical examiner was there, and she sat in a sort of lobby with Nick and held herself stiffly and tried not to think. The Lords of Death were crouched silently at the back of her mind, ready to spring. Nick patted her on the shoulder, trying to reassure her, but he kept looking anxiously toward the door where Maggie had disappeared with Officer Morton. Eventually she reappeared, looking grim, and nodded once to them.

"At least it was quick," she said, with helpless anger in her eyes and voice. "They say she wasn't even bruised." To Mary Beth, the words seemed to have no meaning. Nothing had meaning.

"It was the Triangle Murderer?" Nick asked. He had reached out for Maggie's hand when she appeared, but she had gone unseeing to Mary Beth's other side and now sat down to hold her roommate's hand.

"Yeah. They say it looks like the others," Maggie said. "This guy is impotent about half the time."

"But he didn't beat her?"

"Some are beaten up more thoroughly than others. The only odd thing was that he put her back into the car. Into my car." Her eyes closed and she bit her lip.

"When did it happen?" asked Nick. Keeping her talking.

"This afternoon. They found her by the highway ramp. Like the others. Knifed.'' She frowned, fiercely keeping control of herself. ''It was the same goddamn ramp, Nick.''

''The same as what?''

''The one we could see from the ridge. The one we used this morning. We must have passed within yards of her this afternoon.'' She blinked for a moment and rested her forehead against the palm of her free hand. No, no, I need you, Maggie, don't, thought Mary Beth. Or had she said it out loud? Screamed it so she could be heard above the raucous laughter of Hun-Came? Maggie squeezed her hand and straightened.

''I'll take care of what has to be done, Mary Beth,'' she said. ''Nick, let's see if we can get her a sedative.''

Part of Mary Beth realized that her body was shaking, all on its own.

After a long time, somehow, she was in bed at home, and drowsy. There had been a doctor. There was something bad—it was Jackie, oh God, oh God.

Finally she went to sleep, piece by piece.

She awoke very late Tuesday, to the certain knowledge that the world, so long disintegrating, had finally splintered. She had a headache and couldn't remember quite what had happened for a while, but she also knew she didn't want to remember. She dressed very carefully and brushed her hair slowly. Then she went downstairs.

Sue, Nick, and Maggie were in the kitchen. Maggie was replacing the telephone receiver. ''How are you, Mary Beth?'' she asked.

Mary Beth looked at her vacantly. ''Jackie is dead,'' she explained. ''And I have a headache.''

''He gave you a pretty big dose of sedatives last night,'' Maggie said. ''You're supposed to take this now.'' She handed her a mug of coffee and a pill.

''You got some sleep, at least,'' said Sue sympathetically. The freckled face was puffy, her eyes circled.

Mary Beth sat down and took the pill and drank the coffee in one long draught. She began to pull her mind back into working order. ''We should call her parents,'' she said.

''They're on their way,'' said Maggie. ''The police called them.''

''How about Frank?''

"I spoke to him about an hour or two ago. He wouldn't believe me."

She frowned. "What time is it?"

"Noon."

"I missed my appointment with Greene."

"I called her. You're to call back when you can to make another appointment." Maggie refilled her mug.

The coffee was helping. She said, "Did you get any sleep?"

"Yeah. We sacked out a couple of hours," said Sue. "And we let Nick crash on the sofa."

Mary Beth focused on Nick for the first time and they nodded somberly at each other. Then she asked, "What can I do?"

"I think we'll need help when the family gets here," said Maggie. "Fixing lunch, going through her things with them."

"Okay." She was glad for the promised task. But her head still hurt. There was something, some problem, that she could not endure.

There was pounding at the front door. Sue and Maggie glanced at each other and went to answer, Nick and Mary Beth following.

When Sue unlocked it, Frank exploded into the hallway.

"Okay. Where is she? Where is she?" He looked frantically from one grim face to the other. "Look, I know you're lying. Where is she?"

"Frank, really, we can't believe it either," said Sue. "But it's true. She was killed yesterday."

"You're lying! It can't be! She's not here. None of you saw her!"

"I did, Frank," said Maggie quietly. He stared at her for a long minute.

"You saw her?" he said at last.

"With the police medical examiner."

"The police." He tried to absorb it. "And . . . ?"

"And she was dead, Frank."

"Oh Christ!" He turned away from them, toward the door, and smashed his clenched hand through the glass. He was drawing back his bloodied fist for a second blow when Maggie seized it and twisted his arm back, tapping his legs from under him with a quick kick to the back of his knees. He fell to the floor with a sob. Maggie looked back at them sorrowfully.

"Nick. I think you're the one he needs."

"Okay." Nick was already next to them, quick and quiet, and

now leaned over the younger man, a powerful friendly arm around his shoulders. "Frank, let's take a walk, okay?"

"Oh Christ."

"Come on now." He opened the door and led him out. It was another warm day, Mary Beth saw. Deceptively pleasant, for Aqbal.

The Edwardses, stunned and bewildered, arrived an hour later, and Mary Beth fixed them tea and agreed with everything they said. Mr. Edwards was angry; he soon left for the police station to rage about their inability to capture criminals. Mrs. Edwards tried to sort through her daughter's things, but could not bring herself to stay in Jackie's room more then a few minutes at a time. She finally gave up and said she would try again tomorrow.

Nick stopped by in midafternoon to say that Frank was quieter and had just started back for Syracuse, and that he himself had to get back now for the performance. But he promised to return as soon as he could.

Sue suggested that Mrs. Edwards ought to talk to a funeral director. Mary Beth drove her over in the Land Rover, since Mr. Edwards was still at the police station. She was relieved to see that the practiced compassion of the funeral director had its intended effect; Mrs. Edwards, soothed and coherent, handled the decisions calmly, and said she would check them with her husband.

A few people came by the house, shocked and angry. Sue and Maggie spoke to them, asking that they not talk to reporters. After Mr. Edwards returned and took his wife to their motel room to rest, a little circle of friends formed in the living room—Dan and Peter, Terry and Monica and other WAR members. The police spoke to several of them, trying to find out why Jackie had been driving on the highway, but no one knew.

The group left at last and they opened some tuna fish for a late supper. Maggie went up to take a shower while Sue and Mary Beth straightened up. Mary Beth was picking up the last cups in the living room when there was a knock on the door. It was Nick, who had driven straight over after the show, face and arms still streaked in places with makeup that he had missed in his haste. Sue told him that Maggie was in the shower but she'd go up and tell her. Mary Beth was standing in the living room when he came in.

"Hi, Mary Beth. How are you doing?"

"You lied," she said.

Surprised, he stopped by the chair nearest the door. "When?" he asked.

"You said you weren't her lover."

"That was the truth, Mary Beth."

"You lied." Part of her believed him. Even Maggie had said it was someone else. But a stronger fragment believed he was danger.

"It wasn't a lie." He was puzzled. He tried to read her expression, and continued uncertainly. "But you're right, things have changed. It just doesn't seem like a good time to talk about it."

"You just want to fuck her." She was gripping the Guatemalan blanket on the back of the sofa with both hands.

"You're upset, Mary Beth. Let's talk about something else, okay?"

"You said you were her friend. You aren't. You'll hurt her. Leave her alone!" Why wouldn't he go?

"Please, Mary Beth, let's talk later."

"You just want to fuck her."

He was getting angry. "Goddamnit, Mary Beth, that's not true! There's a hell of a lot more to it! What do you want from me? What the hell are you trying to do?"

He was big, and angry, and she had to protect Maggie from him. Mary Beth was frantic. She braced herself against the sofa and said again, "Leave her alone! You aren't her friend! You just want to fuck her!"

"Mary Beth," said Maggie pleasantly from the door, "shut up or I'll knock your jaw off."

Shocked into silence, Mary Beth stared at her friend. Nick sank wordlessly into the chair and covered his face with his hands.

Mary Beth noticed that she was still gripping the sofa blanket, crushing it in both fists. There were tears starting to run down her face, but she did not feel sad. Maggie crossed the room and hugged her.

"I think it's time to talk, kid," she said softly. Maggie led her around to sit on the sofa, keeping her arm around Mary Beth's shoulders as she spoke to Nick. "Nick, I'll try to take what you said as a compliment, okay? I want to be friends. Just like before. But right now maybe you'd better go."

Nick stood up and Mary Beth stiffened again. He was still angry. He said, "Maggie, look. I know everyone's upset. But I don't know why you're encouraging your so-called friend there in this viciousness. And I think I deserve more than a breezy dismissal."

"You do. It's not a breezy dismissal. It's just that what we have

123

to do will take a while. Please, Nick, try to forgive her. She was raped a while ago, and she hasn't been able to talk about it at all, and she hasn't been able to forget it either. Especially now.''

Just like that, calmly, she said it. Mary Beth shuddered at the simple words.

Nick rubbed a big hand over his head and then said gently, ''Philomel,'' and suddenly he was kneeling in front of her, not frightening anymore, just concerned and friendly. ''Mary Beth, I didn't understand,'' he said. ''Listen, trust Maggie. She'll see you through.'' Mary Beth thought suddenly, What have I done to him? To this gentle man who suffered like me and spoke kindly and gave me hope? She looked away, ashamed. He was standing up again, saying firmly to Maggie, ''I'm going now. But I'll be back tomorrow, Maggie.''

''Okay.''

''Nine o'clock?''

''Okay.''

He went out. Mary Beth whispered, ''Oh God, what did I say to him?''

''He'll be okay,'' said Maggie a bit roughly. ''He'll get a chance to use all this emotion when he's acting sometime.'' She listened, pensive, while the door closed and his car started. Then she led Mary Beth up to her own room, pausing at Sue's door to say, ''Sue, Mary Beth and I have a job to do. Please don't bother us unless it's really important.''

''I never do,'' said Sue, predictably if untruthfully.

Maggie closed the door and sat down on the edge of the bed near Mary Beth. ''Okay. Talk,'' she said, and took her hand.

Mary Beth shook her head. ''I'm so afraid, Maggie.''

''Damn right you're afraid. But it's time to quit hurting yourself. And our friends.''

Mary Beth nodded. ''I'll try. But I'm afraid.''

''Well, I'll be right here with you. Okay? We'll be the Heroic Twins in the underworld and go together. Rivers of blood, and rooms of vampires, and sacrificial knives. Together.''

Mary Beth drew a deep breath and began. And after a few words she found that she'd been wrong, and the Ixil right. You could not erase time. The minutes of that half-hour were clearer than yesterday in her memory, even now.

XIII

6 Aqbal
(January 10, 1968)

Parsonsville, said the little sign. Mary Beth pulled over onto the red clay shoulder and looked at the map. Better get gas here, it would be a long way to the next town. It was four-fifteen now. She could get dinner at McKinley, about ninety miles on.

It was almost wintry here, away from the Tropics, away from the balmy Texas air too. Not cold, but bare, the vegetation resting, tan and still, only a few slow-growing dusty greens. No snow, of course. Not real winter here, even in January. The sun behind high hazy clouds shed flat light on the colorless dead leaves and on the somnolent evergreens. Mary Beth drove slowly into town, past sleepy clapboard houses, looking for gas.

The station was at the crossroads, a broad asphalt area by the highway, a little white-tiled building set far back against a hill. She asked the attendant to fill it and started back toward the rest rooms at the side of the building, modestly shielded by a planting of evergreens. A couple of men in jeans and work shirts were just getting ready to leave, joking as they climbed into pickup trucks. A third, sleeves rolled up, with hair the same rusty brown of a chipmunk on head and chest and forearms, was coming out of the men's room as she went in next door. When she had finished, she washed her hands, looking at her blonde confident image in the cracked mirror, and turned the steel doorknob to start back out to the Land Rover.

The hand came from behind, clamping over mouth and nostrils. She struggled wildly, unable to scream as his fist rammed into ribs and kidneys, and then there was a sudden searing pain that froze her. The other arm, chipmunk-furred, was now pressing a knife point under her left breast. "Quiet, whore," he said softly. "Nobody'll get hurt if you're quiet." He pulled her back behind the station. The knife was long, with a pebbly black handle and a little curve at the tip of the blade. There was a little bit of blood trickling across it. Mine, thought Mary Beth suddenly, my blood. He's going to kill me. I'm going to die. Please God, not yet.

He punched her down into the dead weeds where the gas station building was set into the foot of the hill. It was not tiled on the back, just white stucco with gray stains streaking down from the roof. There was rubble under the weeds, something sharp and lumpy against her back, but that was not important, the knife was important. He had kicked her and moved around on top of her and his hand was not on her mouth anymore, but she could not scream because the knife was still there, solid under her breast. Her blood. She was going to die. He was the Lord of Death, his grunting kept time with the shrieks of silent laughter. I won't scream; at least I can control that, she thought. I'll die with dignity. She closed her eyes. He did something, moved her jeans down, and there was more pain now, in her dry vagina. Dry flesh rasping against her dry softness. But that was not important, the knife was important. Dying with dignity was important. He said over and over, rhythmically, "Quiet, whore. Stupid whore. Stupid whore. Quiet." He had been drinking beer, she could smell it on his breath. I will not scream, she thought. I'll die with dignity. Please God.

After a long time he stopped. He said, "Whore, you tell anyone, I'll kill you. I'll find you. I've got your plate numbers." Then when she was still quiet the knife turned in her wound and he said, "What do you say?"

She lost her dignity and gasped, "I won't tell. Promise."

"Damn right. You're not that stupid, stupid whore."

The knife went away and he stood up. Mary Beth opened her eyes just a crack. He stood straddling her, but he had not zipped his jeans yet, his pubic hair was chipmunk-colored too. Then something hot and liquid slapped her face. Her eyes blinked closed in reflex and it poured over her face and neck and shirt. He was urinating on her. She lay very still because of the knife. There were footsteps going away, a truck starting. She lay still.

After a while the urine was cold, evaporating. She became

aware of the stinging under her breast and the deep harsh burning pain in her genitals.

She was not dead.

Oh dear God, she was not dead.

She opened her eyes. The sky was still pearl-white. The sun was still throwing faint shadows across the hill.

He was gone. He had not killed her.

But he would—he said he would, if she told.

She stood up and looked around. He was really gone.

She was not dead.

She zipped her jeans and hurried around the corner into the rest room and locked the door. She took off her clothes and washed carefully under her breast. She washed her face and hair and genitals. She washed her clothes. There were not enough paper towels. She washed her face and body and genitals again. There was some blood down there too.

He would kill her if she told. He knew her license number.

She put on the wet clothes and combed her hair very carefully. It was a quarter to five. She turned to go out.

She could not.

It was a metal door with chipped white paint and a grubby steel knob. Mary Beth stood, wet and cold, and stared at the steel knob. She began to tremble—first little shivers, then more and more, until she had to lean on the back of the toilet to keep from falling. Then there was a knock on the door.

"You okay, little lady?"

She froze. He was coming to kill her.

But no, that was not his voice. She lunged forward and opened the door and saw the attendant, white-haired, startled. She ran a couple of steps toward her car.

"You okay?"

She still could not answer. She was shivering.

"Looks like you fell in," he commented, concerned, trying to make a joke for her.

"Almost," she said somehow. "How much do I owe you?" She edged toward the Land Rover, away from the dreadful door.

"Four-fifty."

He had not stolen her money. She found a five and gave it to the attendant, and got in the Land Rover and locked the door, and drove off without waiting for the change.

She drove for hours, until her clothes were dry and stiff. She wanted two things, to get away from him, and to wash. In her suitcase were soft dry clothes and lotions. But she was afraid, and kept on driving. When she needed gas she stayed locked in the car, shivering, slotting the window open to slip the money through. Finally, late at night, a consoling thought occurred to her. She had Texas plates on now. When she got to New York, she could get them changed. Then he couldn't find her.

Right now she was approaching Nashville. There was a motel; even this late it said "Vacancy." She turned in, went to the office, and paid for a room. After locking her door, she quickly stripped and stepped into the shower. With lots of soap, she scrubbed herself carefully inside and out. She washed her mouth too, just in case. The soap tasted bitter and clean. Then she dried off carefully and put on soft clean clothes, clean underwear and jeans—and a sweater because it would be colder as she went north. She jammed her polluted clothes into the bathroom wastebasket and washed her hands again. Then she methodically applied cologne to her arms and neck and hair, because the smell of beer and urine wouldn't leave her.

If she told . . . he would kill her.

She stared at the phone a long time and finally snatched it up and called Tip in Arizona and blurted out what had happened. He was angry. He said my God, why did you let him do it? and she said there was a knife and he said how could you do this to me? She said I didn't mean to, and he said intentions don't count, how could you, how could you? So she hung up and put on more cologne and went to the office to pay for the call.

Then she went back to the car and drove north.

Putting it into words had started her shaking all over again. But this time Maggie was there to hold her, and Maggie was saying, "It's so goddamn unfair." The shaking turned into proper sobs which eventually subsided.

After a few minutes she wiped her nose and asked, "Did I do the right thing?"

"Of course."

"Of course?"

"You're alive, dunce. Bright and wonderful and alive."

"But Tip said . . ."

"The hell with Tip!" Maggie hugged her tighter. "God, Mary Beth. No wonder you didn't want to talk."

"Yeah. Yeah, that was it, wasn't it?" Mary Beth was amazed that she hadn't known. It wasn't just the chipmunk man she was afraid of—it was the thought that Tip was right, that it was her fault. "Damn him, Maggie! Damn, damn, damn!"

"Tip really blew it."

"Damn him, he had no right! I believed him, Maggie. Damn!" Hurt, and outraged for the first time, she pounded the mattress beside her.

"Didn't you have other friends you could have told?"

"Well, when I got back here Sue was all full of her own problems too. Paying the rent, finding a new roommate. And also, she's kind of extreme."

"Yeah. She would have got up an army and marched on Parsonsville."

"Probably. Like Sherman to the sea." Mary Beth was surprised to find herself grinning.

"Did you see a doctor?"

"Yes. When I got back here. He said I had syphillis."

"Jesus!"

"Yeah."

"Did you tell him it was rape?"

"No." She sat back a little and pushed a strand of hair from her eyes. "Because he was so goddamn . . . You know what he said?"

"What?"

"Well, he was examining me. You know, very jolly, while that cold steel speculum pries open your vagina?"

"Yeah. I hate that too."

"And he said, 'Well, young lady, one of your boyfriends is pretty rough.' "

"Jesus."

"And he said I'd probably been sleeping around a lot, and wanted to know the names of all my sex partners."

"Didn't he notice your bruises?"

"I told the nurse no breast exam, and so the bruises were mostly under the sheet. He would have thought it was that rough boyfriend, I bet. Anyway, I was probably a simple case for him. Prescribe the penicillin, move on to the next immoral young slut."

"The penicillin cured you?"

"Yeah. At least the symptoms went away."

"Good."

"Do you think I should have told the police?" she asked anxiously.

"I don't know. They might have held you up a long time, maybe for nothing."

"Do you think he would really have killed me?"

"God, Mary Beth, I don't know. He could have, and didn't. But who knows what might have happened if you had stayed around to press charges?"

"I feel bad for the other women he'll get."

"Sure. But you probably weren't the first, and he was out loose, right? Anyway, if you'd lived there, it would have made more sense to call the police. I mean, he probably has friends there. You don't. It would have been very hard for you."

"I see what you mean. I didn't even know his name."

"It's Tip that makes me mad."

"Yeah. He sure didn't help."

"I wonder why? Did he seem okay before?"

"Yeah." It seemed so long ago now. "We were . . . I thought we were very close. We had a lot of fun. Laughed at the same things. He was really interested in my work, and I was interested in what he was doing."

"Well, I guess when you called you hadn't seen each other for a while."

"We'd written. But it doesn't matter. I can't believe now I was ever in love with him. I just feel numb about him. Except for one thing."

"What?"

"It's hard to explain. It's just that when it happened, it didn't have anything to do with sex, or anything like that. The guy was just attacking me in general, you know what I mean? Like a mugging. I didn't even think about sex, I was just afraid he'd kill me. He was like the Lords of Death."

"Yeah. He was."

"Sex was just one more way to attack me. But then when Tip said those things, it suddenly got more important. It wasn't just a mugging anymore. Tip made me think somehow it was my fault—that no one could love me, and I couldn't love anyone."

"God, Mary Beth."

"Once you said to me, enjoy your immunity. Remember?"

"I'm sorry. Jesus, I'm sorry, Mary Beth. Old salt-in-the-wound Ryan."

"Well, you were right. I haven't had any sexual feelings for months, Maggie. I'm just not interested anymore."

"Not at all?"

"No. And I keep thinking all men are like that. Frank. Even . . . oh, Maggie, even Nick. Tonight."

"You were trying to protect me." There was an odd smile on Maggie's face.

"Yeah. Something like that. Oh God, Maggie, can you ever forgive me? Can he?"

"Yeah. He's pretty understanding. But please tell your subconscious to leave Nick and me alone in the future." There was grimness in her voice.

"I promise, honest. But Maggie, do you think I'll ever be normal again?"

"Normal? Hell, Mary Beth, what do I know about normal?"

"Yeah. I don't know either." She thought a minute. "I still love people. My mom and my sister, and Ros in Guatemala, and you and Sue and Jack—Jackie. Oh, God, why are we talking about me when Jackie is dead?"

"It was time to talk. It's no disrespect to Jackie."

"I wonder how it happened to her? Why was she there, on that ramp?"

"Who knows? Coming to find us at the park? Or to visit Frank in Syracuse? I don't know why she started that cake, though. God, I still can't believe it happened to her, of all people."

Mary Beth nodded. There was a feeling of weariness and peace and of enormous sorrow for Jackie seeping into her. And something else, something unfamiliar.

"I'm hungry," she said, astonished.

"So am I," Maggie replied, smiling a little.

"Nick says you always are."

"Damn Nick!" said Maggie with unnecessary vehemence. "Let's go eat something." She pulled Mary Beth roughly to her feet and they went down to fix toasted cheese sandwiches. And to talk about Jackie and cry.

XIV

11 Kach
(June 19, 1968)

At first the police had not released Jackie's name to the press, but now that they had seen Mr. and Mrs. Edwards, they were giving out the information. On Wednesday, shortly after seven a.m., the telephone began to shrill. Maggie answered in the upstairs hall as Mary Beth and Sue came sleepily to their doors.

"Hello? . . . No, I'm sorry, you have the wrong number . . . No, there's no one of that name here . . . No . . . No . . . Good-bye." The receiver slammed down.

"Wrong number?" asked Sue.

"No. Press. Listen, if anyone asks about Jackie, this is not the right place. Okay? Her parents will be back today and they shouldn't be hassled."

"Of course not. And neither should we," said Sue indignantly.

The phone rang again. Maggie picked it up. "Hello? . . . No, you must have the wrong number . . . Okay, good-bye." She replaced the receiver. "That one was more polite, at least. Okay if I take it off the hook?"

"Please do," said Sue.

They fixed breakfast—a bleak affair. The news of Jackie's death was on the local radio. Mary Beth switched it off. She felt exhausted and sad and angry at the insane world. And also, for the first time in months, worthwhile.

The Edwardses arrived at eight-fifteen and went together to Jackie's room. They could hear Mrs. Edwards sobbing occasionally. Two or three friends came by briefly, apologetically, saying

132

they had heard the news on the radio but couldn't get through on the phone. Sue confirmed the news, explained about the press, and asked them to come back in the afternoon.

Nick arrived at nine, as promised. Maggie, opening the door, greeted him calmly.

Mary Beth, who had heard them from upstairs, ran down and went to him. "Nick. I'm very, very sorry."

"Don't worry about it, Mary Beth. You seem better now."

"Yes. I was very upset last night. I'm sorry."

"I know you were. And you were trying to take care of Maggie."

So he did understand. She smiled at him, a rather wobbly smile. Maggie said, almost humorously, "We've agreed that in the future I'm to defend myself from your onslaughts by myself."

"I see." His serious brown eyes met her unexpectedly defiant blue ones and he nodded. "Yes, I see. Look, I want to help, if I can. What needs to be done?"

Maggie moved restlessly to the living room window to look out. "Little things, mostly. Jackie's parents are here going through her things. They might need help. The press is after us. We're running out of coffee." She turned back to them. "The funeral will be in New Jersey, but we'll have a memorial service here Friday."

"I'd like to come."

"If you want."

"What brand of coffee do you use?"

"Cheapest."

"Okay, I'll go . . ."

He stopped as Mrs. Edwards came sobbing down the stairs. Mary Beth hurried to her. "Come on, now. Let's have a cup of tea," she said soothingly.

"I just can't manage," Mrs. Edwards said brokenly.

"It's good to cry. Come on." She took her to Sue in the kitchen. When she returned Nick and Maggie were standing silently at opposite ends of the sofa. His grave eyes were on her as she fingered the fringe of the blanket.

The doorbell rang, followed by loud knocking. Maggie, as though released, ran out to answer it.

"Yes?"

"Chip Hunter, from the *Eagle,* ma'am. We're after some background on the latest Triangle murder. This is where the dead girl lived? This, um, Jacqueline Edwards?"

133

"Oh no. You have the wrong place."

"This is the address we were given."

"Oh no. This is the Eternal Light Commune now." Maggie's voice was breathless and sincere. Eyes widening, Mary Beth went to look into the hall. In the living room behind her, Nick began, inexplicably, to take off his shoes.

"You mean this Edwards girl moved?"

"She must have moved, yes."

"Are you sure? This is the exact address, 519 Walton." The reporter was pushing forward, straining to see behind Maggie into the house. Two more strangers with tape recorders were starting up the walk.

"Oh no," said Maggie with a sort of breathless serenity. "You are mistaken."

"No, my daughter," came a ringing mellow voice. "He is not mistaken. No one who knocks on this door is mistaken."

Mary Beth, amazed, looked back to see Nick sweeping the Guatemalan blanket off the sofa and around his shoulders. He strode, gracefully draped and barefoot, into the hall.

Maggie didn't even blink. She said, "You are right, of course, Father Nicholas."

"He is not mistaken," continued Nick warmly. "The Great Lord, the Eternal Light, has sent him. He is a Seeker." In the blanket he looked immense. His benevolent brow and kind voice set off the hard, frightening gleam of his half-closed eyes.

The *Eagle* reporter almost stepped on one of his fellows as he backed away from the door. He said, "Christ!"

"Yes. Some call Him Christ, some call Him Buddha," agreed Nick in that deep hypnotic voice. "And there are many other names. All seek Him. As you do, my son, am I not correct?"

"Look, I'm just trying to find Jacqueline Edwards's house."

"No, my son. Do not battle your happy fate. Do not leave," said Nick, stepping after him onto the porch. His dark eyes gleamed fanatically under half-closed lids.

Maggie followed them out, hand extended in appeal. "Please, do not leave, my brothers! Father Nicholas is right. You were sent!"

Mary Beth suddenly noticed that her own mouth was open. She closed it abruptly.

"Please, my sons," said Nick, rocking up a little on his bare feet, and looking huge and splendid in the blanket. "You must

134

yield to the Divine Power that sent you here. Am I correct that you represent our newspapers? Am I correct that you could let the people hear of our efforts here at the Eternal Light Commune? Behold!'' An impressive finger shot skyward. "Behold our symbols! The pierced pane!'' He turned in a swirl of blanket, eyes glittering, and indicated the window Frank had smashed. "Symbol of the pure life further purified by the entrance of Divine Light!''

One of the reporters had already slipped away. The other two now turned and left. One muttered, "Thanks a lot, Father Nicholas," before his car door slammed.

"Please, my sons, do not defy the Divine Power!'' There was deep regret in the mellow voice that rolled after them as they drove away.

Mary Beth, a bit staggered, moved back into the hall and sat down abruptly on the stairs. Nick stalked in with priestly gait, but the hard, glistening eyes had become mild and merry again. Maggie turned to the mailbox she had been leaning against and began scratching out all their names viciously and writing something on it. She came in after a minute and closed the door. Nick took off his blanket.

"Hot little costume, Father Nicholas," said Maggie a touch unsteadily.

"Certainly is," he agreed.

"Yes. Mary Beth, until further notice we're the Eternal Light Commune.''

"Jeez," said Mary Beth.

"Yes. Some call Him Jeez," mimicked Maggie, and then seemed to choke a little. She turned abruptly to hide her face against the corner of the wall. "Oh, holy shit, Nick!''

"That's what it was, all right," he agreed gravely.

Mary Beth giggled, then said, "Tartuffe."

"Yes. One of my secret yens is to play that role." He grinned and took the blanket back into the living room, and arranged it carefully on the sofa again. Mary Beth followed him in.

"Did you two plan that?" she asked, puzzled.

"Of course not." He pulled on his socks and smiled at her. "I see there are sides of Maggie you still haven't discovered."

"Well, I guess we've had a few hints," she admitted, thinking of the alarm clocks, and of Birgit Nilsson, and of the dowdy Maggie who had eased Frank into Jackie's arms. Poor Frank. Poor Jackie. A little sob slipped through her tight throat.

135

"Are you all right?"

"Just thinking of Jackie. You know." She snuffled.

"Yes. It catches you unawares sometimes." He took her hand. "I heard you tell Mrs. Edwards it's good to cry. You're right, you know."

She nodded as he patted her hand. In a moment she took a deep breath, swallowed, and said, "I should let you get your other shoe on."

"Oh, no, I left it off on purpose," he said. "I have a little project on the front porch."

"What?"

"Well, you're 519 Walton right now. I think maybe for a little while you should be 516."

"Hey. Brilliant!"

"That's me," he said cheerfully.

They went back into the hall. Maggie was exactly as they had left her, leaning against the wall in the corner, face hidden. Nick paused, worried, holding his shoe. Mary Beth hurried to her.

"Hey. Hey, Maggie."

"Yeah?" She didn't move.

"Hey, come on. Is it Jackie? Come on in the living room."

"Okay." She straightened up but her hands still hid her face.

Nick said, "Maggie, I'm going to fix the house number and get some coffee. And then I won't be back for a while. Okay?"

"Okay." She raised ravaged blue eyes to him and said, "If nothing else comes up I'll try to say a civil good-bye later this week. You've caught me at a bad time."

"I know."

He watched, gripping the shoe, while Mary Beth led her to the living room sofa, and then he went out and rehung the number, using the heel of his shoe as a hammer. In a few minutes they heard his car start. Maggie sat huddled on the sofa, uncharacteristically still.

Mary Beth put her hand on the hunched bony shoulder and asked, "Maggie, what's wrong?"

"Let's see," said Maggie, considering the question solemnly and enumerating on her fingers. "There's Jackie. There's you. There's Vietnam, and Guatemala, and Martin Luther King, and riots, and Bobby Kennedy. Dr. Spock is going to jail. And a couple of personal things. I'm out of fingers. Shall I start on my toes?"

"Never mind," said Mary Beth. "I'll bring you some tea."

XV

11 Kach
(June 19, 1968)

The day wore on. Mr. and Mrs. Edwards left eventually, and later that afternoon Maggie, Mary Beth, and several visitors sat in the living room drinking iced tea. People had been collecting all afternoon, talking quietly about other things to fill the emptiness, and when Sue brought in the big pitcher and glasses, there was quite an assembly. Frank had returned, measured the windowpane, bought glass, and silently replaced it. Peter had come over too, and sat quietly in a chair, clicking his ballpoint pen in and out. Terry and Monica were there, as were Bill and Todd from across the street—awkward but genuinely sympathetic. They were just preparing to leave when Sue arrived with fresh provisions.

"Have some iced tea and sandwiches before you go," she suggested, putting the tray down. Bill started to decline.

"Actually," said Maggie, "there's something you can help with, if you stay."

"Sure," said Bill eagerly. "What?"

"Well, it's just that it seems crazy that we can't figure out what she was doing."

"What do you mean?"

"When Jackie borrowed my car, she said she needed it to take books to the library. She didn't say a word about going to Syracuse."

"Yeah. That's not like her," said Sue.

"All I know is, I waited for her an hour in the library," said Peter miserably.

137

"Yes. When was she supposed to meet you?"

"At four. We'd arranged it back, oh, Wednesday, I think."

"And she said nothing about not being able to make it?"

"Nothing at all. I called here at four-thirty to check."

"Yeah, I remember," said Sue.

"Okay," said Maggie. "So it looks like something had already gone wrong by then. I saw her last at eleven. Right, Mary Beth?"

"Yes. Maybe a few minutes later."

"And do you remember what she said then?"

"That she had a date at the library, so she couldn't go on the picnic."

"That's right," said Sue.

"Okay. Now let's go on. Sue, you and she were in the house alone for a while."

"And both working like dogs, not gamboling in the sun like you frivolous things."

Maggie made a face at her. "Try to restrain these personal attacks for a few minutes, Comrade Snyder. Did you see her at all, or hear her, while you slaved away?"

"Let's see. I grabbed a sandwich for lunch, and she came down after a few minutes. Looked into the refrigerator and groused because you'd used up all the tomatoes." Her gruffness was masking the pain of remembering.

"Guess I had," said Maggie regretfully. "Needed them for the beef daube."

"Then she started fixing herself some lunch. I had finished eating so I went back up to work."

"Okay."

"She came up after a few minutes and made a phone call."

"Who to?"

"I don't know. I was busy. I did hear her say, 'So everyone will be gone at two-thirty?' and then 'Fine, see you soon.' And then she hung up."

"Interesting." Maggie held out a page torn from the telephone notepad. "This seems to be her note about it: '2:30 LB.' "

"Yeah. That would be it," agreed Sue. "Unless Mary Beth made that note."

Mary Beth shook her head.

Maggie was frowning at the note. "Any idea what LB means?"

"Library," suggested Sue.

"Probably. Except it's not empty at two-thirty."

138

"Parts of it are. The Georgian room?"

"Yeah."

Mary Beth looked over Maggie's shoulder. She said, "They're both capital letters. Could they be initials?"

"Possible. A person? A place?"

They thought a while. Barnes, Brown. Someone thought of Lydia Bondini, and someone else suggested Lake Bowman, thirty miles east. Finally Maggie said dubiously, "There's Professor Berryman."

A funny look came across Frank's face. "Berryman?"

"Lincoln Berryman," Maggie repeated. "Psych department."

"Oh God. But that couldn't be it."

"What, Frank?"

"Well, Jackie said it was best not to say anything about it. And it may not mean anything."

"Frank . . . ," Maggie said encouragingly.

"Well, a couple of months ago . . . I'd just met her Friday afternoon. We were going out for dinner. She wanted to borrow a paper from Professor Freeman to use on her project. It was pretty late, and the door was closed, but she knocked anyway. Professor Freeman said come in, but when Jackie opened the door Professor Freeman was looking very upset, and this big guy was standing there looking upset too. I think Professor Freeman referred to him as Professor Berryman."

"Dark hair? Beard? Pretty heavy, but not really fat?"

"Yes."

"That's him," said Maggie. "What else?"

"That's it. When we'd left Jackie said it looked like we'd interrupted something, but, you know, faculty private lives aren't really our business. I don't think she ever mentioned it to anyone, and I certainly didn't."

"And Professor Freeman told you to come in?"

"Yes. Loud and quick."

"Well, it doesn't sound like it was anything she was ashamed of," said Sue. "I still vote for the library."

"Yeah. I agree," said Frank.

"Well, okay," said Maggie. "What happened after the phone call, Sue?"

"She muttered, 'Damn, I'll have to come back.' Then she went to her room and I got back to work."

"What time was all this?"

"Oh, maybe twelve-thirtyish."

"Okay. What next?"

"I don't remember anything else for the next hour, except for Dostoyevsky."

"Okay, we needn't go into that."

"Philistine! Then she went downstairs again and messed around in the kitchen. Probably working on that unspeakable cake. Then she started out the front door and yelled up that she'd be back soon. And that's the last I ever saw her."

"What time did she leave?"

"Two-fifteen, maybe. Not much earlier."

"Two-fifteen."

"Right."

"And she didn't say anything about Syracuse?"

"Not one damn word."

"Okay." Maggie was frowning. "Did she take my car then, or walk?"

"I don't know. I was slaving away over that Cyrillic novel—not listening at all." Sue turned away from them and Maggie's hand found hers consolingly.

Bill said, "Was that her in your car?"

"Yes," said Maggie, "if you're talking about Monday."

"Yeah. I think we saw her leave. Todd and I were picking up the lawn. Beer cans and stuff, you know, from the party. 'Cause we were too hung over to do it Sunday. Remember, Todd?"

"Yeah." Todd looked uncomfortable.

"I remember because I thought it was you. We couldn't really see who was driving. And Todd said we ought to shoot out her god-damn tires. Remember, Todd?"

Todd scowled, but Maggie grinned and said, "Well, thanks for your restraint. Did she go toward campus?"

"Yes," said Bill.

"Okay. Did anybody see her at all after two-fifteen?"

Everyone looked glumly at everyone else.

"Well, let's try a process of elimination. She wasn't here; we know that. Peter, you were in the library at four to meet her."

"Yes, actually I was there a little earlier. We were going to go up to the graduate reading room, but I had to check something in the catalog first. So I was there about a quarter of, and went upstairs about four."

"And there was no sign of her, upstairs or down?"

140

"No, none at all."

Monica said, "I was in the reading room all afternoon. She wasn't there. I did see Peter come in about four, and leave at four-thirty and then come back maybe ten minutes later."

"That was when he phoned here, I guess."

"Right," said Peter.

"Okay. So if she was there she gave everyone the slip. But it's possible, it's a big place. What I don't understand is why she'd arrange to be there at two-thirty and then again at four. Why not just stay? Make the appointments closer together, after the cake was out?"

"Yes, or ask Sue to take the cake out," said Mary Beth. "Unless she didn't want to impose."

"Oh, that won't wash, Mary Beth," said Sue. "You know damn well that every one of you dump your responsibilities in my lap. I've taken out zillions of crappy cakes in the last few months!"

"Gastronomy aside," said Maggie, "you're right. She was better organized than that. If she expected to be back in time, she would be. If not, she'd ask you to take it out."

"Maybe," said Mary Beth dubiously, "she met whoever it was at two-thirty, and then forgot all about the cake and just stayed at the library, thinking Peter would be there soon."

"Then why didn't Peter or I see her?" asked Monica.

Mary Beth had already cooled to her idea. "Anyway, that still doesn't explain why she was driving to Syracuse," she said.

Everyone looked at Frank. He said violently, "I can't think of a damn thing! I was home most of that time, I was typing my damn bibliography. She knew that, knew I'd be home, so maybe if she thought of some reason she'd come to see me. But she's never done that before. We've always talked on the phone first."

"And," said Peter defiantly, "she's never stood me up." He and Frank exchanged hostile looks.

Maggie ignored the undertones. "You're right," she said. "She was always reliable. It really looks like her plans had nothing to do with Syracuse. Put in the cake. Go to the two-thirty thing. Come back and take out the cake. The box said it should bake fifty to sixty minutes, all right? So the two-thirty thing was supposed to be short. Then, after the cake, she was going to go back to meet Peter."

"And instead," said Mary Beth, "whatever she did at two-thirty, or just before or just after, made her decide to go to Syracuse without telling anyone first. Made her forget the cake and maybe even Peter?''

"Must have been earth-shattering," said Maggie. "But I still think she would have called Peter if she could have. Were you home, Peter?''

"Yeah, until three-thirty."

"She could've called, then. So whatever the news was, it made her hurry. Couldn't stop for anything. So why would she stop for a guy on a highway ramp?''

Sue said slowly, "Do you think he was the one she met at two-thirty? Do you think he lives around here?''

The question had been hovering in many of their minds.

"You mean someone was actually out to murder her? Made an appointment with her?" Peter was shaking his head. "That's impossible. No one could hate Jackie.''

"Rapists hate females, period," said Sue.

"She was in my car," said Maggie, her expression coolly blank, and Mary Beth suddenly understood the source of the frustration and guilt that had been dogging her friend these past few days. "Maybe somebody hated me." She didn't look at Todd.

Mary Beth said, "It was a knife, Maggie. It couldn't be mistaken identity.''

A flash of gratitude. "Yeah. I keep telling myself that," she said. "And there are other problems too. For example, how would he force her to drive my car to Syracuse, if he had to be in his?''

"Maybe he lives around here like Sue said. Maybe she knew him, believed his story.''

"But if she was conned, she still would have called Sue and Peter before driving off. She was always thoughtful.''

"Maybe he drove. Brought her along, tied up or something," suggested Terry.

"But then how did he get away? He left the car, with her in it.''

"Maybe he lives in Schellsburg.''

"But that just gives you the same problem in reverse," said Mary Beth. "Instead of how he got away, you have to explain how he got here in the first place.''

"Hitch?" suggested Peter.

"Possible," agreed Maggie dubiously. "But it's an odd way of working. The women lived all over the Syracuse area. So he'd have to figure out a way home from somewhere, some exit ramp.

142

He'd hitch to where he could kidnap the woman in her own car, then he'd drive her to his escape point. Kill her and escape.''

Mary Beth considered this plan. She was surprised at her own detachment. "Well," she said, "maybe. But it seems like a lot of unnecessary work for the guy. He wouldn't want to get caught. Simpler would be safer. What if the person he hitched with remembered him?''

"I know. I don't like it much either. It looks as though he's just picked them off the highway at random,'' said Maggie. "But then we're back to the other problem. Why was Jackie going to Syracuse, in such a hurry that she didn't tell us?''

"Were any of the other women in unexpected places?'' asked Monica.

No one knew.

"Maybe we should talk to the police again. Find out if he ever worked that way,'' suggested Terry.

"Good idea,'' said Maggie. "Let's do that. But if he didn't work that way, it's up to us. Why was she driving to Syracuse? And what was she doing at two-thirty? Because this guy has got to be stopped.''

Everyone nodded in vehement agreement. There were no further suggestions, so Sue and Terry volunteered to go talk to Professor Freeman and ask her to call the police to find out if the murderer left his victims in unexpected places. They left, and the rest of the group broke up too. Mary Beth and Maggie straightened up disconsolately, and went up to their rooms to try to work. But it was almost impossible. Mary Beth decided to work on vocabulary cards, because they did not require continuous thought. After an hour or so she went downstairs, fixed some more iced tea, and carried two glasses upstairs.

"Maggie?'' she called through the closed door.

"Yeah?''

"Here's iced tea, if you want it.''

The door opened and Maggie took the glass gratefully. "Thanks,'' she said.

"Getting much done?'' asked Mary Beth.

"Of course not.''

"I'm not either.''

"I just can't believe that guy caught her. Not after the discussions we've had. How the hell does he trap women like that? What trick does he use?''

"I don't know. It seems impossible, if they're in their own cars." She'd never get out of the car alone again.

"Yeah. And then I keep thinking about Frank and Peter," Maggie admitted. "I feel for them. And for her parents."

"We all loved her, Maggie."

"I know. Of course I know. But some kinds of love are especially potent."

"Yeah, guess so." Mary Beth tried to remember how she had felt about Tip, but she still couldn't. It seemed so irrelevent.

"And it reminds me of things," Maggie added in a low tone. She turned away quickly and sat on her bed, holding the cold glass in both hands. Little drops formed on it and slid down onto her jeans.

"You're thinking of what Nick went through?"

"Yes, partly."

Mary Beth considered a moment. "It probably won't be quite as bad for Frank and Peter," she said. "We're doing half."

"Mary Beth, you're as clear as mud."

"I mean, they loved her the way Nick loved his wife, maybe. But they didn't live with her. We're the ones who'll be noticing the empty chairs and missing her voice and so on."

Maggie gave her an odd look. "That will make it easier for them, you think? Never really being used to having her around?"

"Well, I don't know if it will. It just seems that way to me."

"Could be. I've never really been around either of the people I miss most. But maybe I'd miss them even more if I had been."

"Maybe."

Maggie stood up laboriously, as though it required all her strength. "Well, back to work, if work is the right word for it."

"Okay."

"Thanks for the tea and sympathy."

Mary Beth went back to her room, and actually managed to get all the way through the K's.

Jane looked up at the knock on her open office door. "Oh, hi, Sue, Terry."

"Hi. We were just talking about Jackie."

"Yes." Jane turned toward them sympathetically. It must be hard for these young people, losing a close friend. "You must be upset. We all are. It's unbelievable."

"I know," said Terry. "And we wondered if you would do us a

144

favor. Because we couldn't figure out why she was going to Syracuse. And we thought maybe she might have been kidnapped here."

"Here?" A frightening thought. "You mean the Triangle Murderer is here? Surely not!"

"No, no. Just that he goes to where he can kidnap someone and drives them to an escape point."

"That's possible, I suppose."

"Well, we wondered if you would call Sergeant Rayburn for us, see if he can tell us if the guy might have operated that way."

"Right now?"

"Instantly!" said Sue. "Well, you know."

Jane smiled. "Okay. You want to know if there is evidence that he might have met her here, forced her to drive to that exit, and then . . . what? Was his own car here, or there?"

"Oh, it's a screwy idea. We thought maybe he hitched here, or something."

"Well," said Jane dubiously, "I could ask. But it seems a strange theory."

"Yeah. The only good thing about it is that it would mean Jackie didn't go there of her own free will. Because everything else we know seems to show that she was planning to stay in town."

"I see. It was a nice day, though. Couldn't she just have decided on a drive?"

Sue shook her head determinedly. "That just wouldn't be like her. She would have said something. And anyway, I heard her turn down an invitation to go to the park that very day."

"Maybe she changed her mind. People aren't a hundred percent predictable, you know. If they were, we psychologists would be out of a job."

"Oh, I know. But, you see, she had these two appointments. That was odd too. In the library, one at two-thirty and one at four. And she left for the two-thirty and never showed for the four o'clock."

"I see." That was puzzling.

"So maybe she heard some news at the two-thirty meeting that made her want to go to Syracuse." Jane was silent, pondering, and Sue added, "I wish we knew who she met, what they talked about. We're just guessing."

"What news could she get to make her want to go there?"

"Hell, I don't know!" exploded Sue. "I wouldn't entertain that

145

other half-assed idea if there was a reasonable reason for her to go to Syracuse! But there just isn't!"

"I see," said Jane. "I see your point. Both theories have problems. But it still seems more likely to me that she decided to go, for some reason."

"Well, you didn't live with her. It's just not like her. She was a very thoughtful person."

"Yes, I see. Well, let me call Rayburn." She picked up the phone and was put through, amazingly, right away. When she finished talking to him, she hung up and turned back to Sue and Terry.

"He says the Triangle Murderer doesn't work that way," she said bluntly. "No sign of kidnapping in any of the other cases."

"All those women were where they were supposed to be?"

"Well, they were all driving alone. A few hadn't left specific word about where they were going, but the locations weren't unusual for them. And most were on the ramp you'd expect, given the work or the errands they were doing."

"So," said Sue unhappily, "that's that. We're stuck with believing that she suddenly decided to go to Syracuse."

"It seems most likely," said Jane.

They left. But Jane sat frowning for a few minutes. Sue and Terry were right; it didn't quite fit.

Suppose you followed through with the line of thought they'd suggested. Suppose the Triangle Murderer really was from here. Were there any reasonable suspects? University people could come and go with more freedom than those in most other occupations. Did anyone here seem troubled enough to do such things? Linc, who considered his wife unsympathetic? Dick Davies, with those knives under his bed? Students unhappy with grades, or unbalanced, or drunk? Josh, in his constant benevolent chemical haze? Jane shook her head. They all seemed possible, but unlikely. There was no way to figure it out. And if her own department had that many possibilities, and there were dozens of departments, it would be a needle in a haystack. No, they'd have to wait until the Triangle Murderer made a mistake, and he seemed to be a very careful man.

It was depressing, an extra problem she wished she didn't have to worry about. The thought of suicide flickered before her eyes, but she took a Valium instead.

* * *

Toward the end of that busy, grieving week, Mary Beth took stock.

Breaking her silence hadn't been a magic cure, of course. She still grieved deeply about Jackie, and her own problems lingered on. There were still nightmares. She was still numb about sex. The flashes still came at the unexpected glimpse of a stucco wall or a steel doorknob. But the spasms of despair were lessening, and her appetite came back occasionally. And Friday, drying off after her shower, she discovered that she no longer seemed to reek of beer and urine. When she came down to dinner, smelling only of Ivory soap, Maggie smiled and gave Mary Beth's hand a squeeze.

She resolved to start going to WAR meetings. There was talk of starting a crisis counseling service. Maybe, she thought, if I'd had someone to call, I wouldn't have felt so worthless for quite so long.

She had done the right things. Tip was wrong. In an uncontrollable situation, she had been intelligent. She had endured. Like Ros. Like the Heroic Twins.

In the back of her mind, hope, fragil as a snowdrop, began to bloom through her sorrow for her friend. Hope that someday she would again feel in control of her life.

Hope that was nearly destroyed on Saturday.

XVI

1 Chee
(June 22, 1968)

Mary Beth yawned. She was sitting in Maggie's car, watching the fields roll by. "Exit 14 Ahead," said the sign. Another twenty minutes. Nick was going to buy them an early supper before his final show. He'd be leaving for New York tomorrow and had finally convinced Maggie to see him. She had insisted that Mary Beth come along too. A long drive on a warm afternoon, but a welcome change from the tense flurry that had surrounded Jackie's memorial service. Mary Beth yawned again.

"Oh Christ," said Maggie suddenly. "The hummingbird trick!"

"What?" murmured Mary Beth.

"Get down quick, Mary Beth. Backseat on the floor." Her voice was firm and cool.

"Why?"

"Because if you don't I'll pass a magnet all over your Ixil tapes," said Maggie levelly.

Mary Beth started to smile but suddenly realized she was serious. "You mean it!" A nibble of terror brought her full awake.

"Humor me, kid. Get down back there and don't move."

"But . . ."

"Shut up!"

Mary Beth scrambled back into the dusty hollow between the front and back seats, shoving back books and shoes and tools out of her way. A second later Maggie's raincoat dropped over her. She felt the car swerve and slow, then reverse briefly and stop. There

148

was the scent of clover through the open windows. The driver's door opened, slammed again.

"Hi," said Maggie's bright voice from the outside. "Got a problem?"

"Yeah, this little kitten ran out in front of my car. I swerved and hit the rail, but I'm afraid I bumped him a little." A man talking, pleasant and apologetic. "I picked him up to take him to a vet, but now the car's wobbling and I'm afraid to go any farther."

"Tough luck." Maggie's sympathetic voice was farther away now. "Poor little fellow."

"Could you give us a lift?" He was just outside. Mary Beth lay very still in the musty darkness under the raincoat.

"Why don't I just take a look at your car? Where's your key?"

Oh God, Maggie, you fool, you goddamn fool.

"No, don't bother, you could just give me a lift to a vet. I'll call the service station from there."

"I'm pretty good with motors," Maggie declared. "Maybe it's safe to drive. That would save you a lot of trouble." She was still far away, still cheerful. Mary Beth, despairing, could think only of the Lords of Death.

"I know a vet on South Salina," he said. "You could just drop me there. Hey, what are you doing?" There was a faint creak of metal.

"Just opening your hood. Can't see much with it closed, can we?"

"Listen, get your hands off my car!" His voice, not so pleasant now, retreated toward hers.

"Golly, I'm just trying to help. No need to get upset."

"Listen, I don't want anyone monkeying with my car!"

"I'm not touching your car. I'm just looking." They were both distant now. Mary Beth had to strain to hear the conversation.

"All I wanted was a ride! Won't you help the kitten?"

"The kitten isn't in pain. And you won't need a ride if it's safe to drive. Right?"

"Keep your hands off it!"

Mary Beth edged her head up cautiously, looking around carefully. She stopped when she could just see them, several yards farther up the ramp. They were standing by the open hood of a gray Chevrolet parked under a tree at the side of the ramp. At the upper end of the ramp the highway traffic roared by. Maggie's hands were raised, open, in a gesture of innocence.

149

"I'm not touching your car. See?"

The man looked at her uncertainly, the kitten limp in his hands. The hummingbird trick, she'd said.

"If you would let me touch it, I could check a couple of things," she continued. "Why don't you get in and start it? Not much exterior damage. It may be okay."

He was not a particularly tall man, only an inch or so taller than Maggie, but he was heavy and muscular. He wore jeans and a brown striped shirt. Now he suddenly glanced back in Mary Beth's direction. For an instant she feared he'd seen her, frozen there in the back, but he seemed to be looking at the side of the road next to the cars. He suddenly took his decision, set the kitten in the grass, and moved away from Maggie to the passenger side of the hood. He pointed to the motor.

"Look, could that be it?"

"The alternator? I doubt it. Wouldn't make it wobble."

"No. I mean under there." He was still pointing.

Maggie glanced up at the highway and back toward her own car as she walked around the front of his. Mary Beth risked a glance through the side window. An abrupt drop of several feet beyond the shoulder of the road next to their car. Trees and bushes. Anyone down there could not be seen from the highway.

Maggie arrived next to him, watching him now. He said, "Down there." And very deliberately, she leaned over to look into the engine.

The knife was out instantly against her ribs, and his other hand seized her hand, pressing it up behind her to her shoulder blades. Mary Beth felt faint. She sank back under the raincoat.

"Ouch! What are you doing?" Maggie sounded annoyed.

"Come on, bitch. Just walk quiet."

"Look, I was only trying to help! No sense getting mad."

"Shut up. I'm in charge, not you. Just walk along."

"Are you taking me back to my car? Listen, I'll go, you've convinced me. You don't have to do the tough act."

"Just walk along."

"Okay, okay, I'm walking. What the hell do you want?"

Their footsteps were very close now.

"Just walk. Now down."

"Down? Uh!" There was a sudden scrambling sound outside. Mary Beth tensed under the raincoat.

"I don't . . . mmmph!" Her voice was suddenly cut off.

So Maggie too, her bold bright friend, her hope and prop, had been broken. The Lords of Death had won again.

What would I do if I were free, in control, if I could choose? Mary Beth wondered numbly. Maybe pick up this wrench. Open the door quietly so he wouldn't notice. Check the approaches for cover. If I were free.

She picked up the wrench, opened the door, and checked for cover. He'd be hiding from the highway, so there would be bushes screening them from that side. Keeping low, she crept behind the car, down into the bushes, slowly. There was the sound of a scuffle, twigs breaking. She stayed low. They were just ahead now.

A branch jabbed her cheek. She thought, Jesus, I'm as big a fool as she is.

Then there was no time for thought. She saw them through the lattice of branches and blowing leaves. They were in profile, Maggie on her back, legs braced against the ground. He was bent over her, one knee on her stomach. His left hand was clamped across her mouth and nose, hard. But the problem was clearly the knife. Both of Maggie's hands were on his right forearm. He was pushing the blade toward her neck; she was pushing his arm away. Their muscles strained, his thick arm bulging, Maggie's leaner, smoother arms taut with effort too. She moved a knee clumsily against his side and he shifted suddenly and rammed his weight against it, pinning her leg to the ground. She had not faltered in the pressure on his knife hand, but he had loosened his grip on her mouth an instant as his weight shifted, and Mary Beth heard her suck in a great breath before his hand pressed down again.

Mary Beth thought coolly. Nick had said wham him quick.

Shifting sideways and checking for quiet footing, she found a place where she could emerge right behind him. She chose the spot, right on the back of the head, stood up, and lunged. She struck just in time, it seemed, because Maggie's pained blue eyes were flickering and her strong gymnast's arms suddenly slackening. The knife was already slicing through the side of Maggie's plaid shirt when Mary Beth slammed the wrench into the man's skull.

He collapsed instantly. Maggie heaved him off and bounced to her feet, gasping. For a moment they both stood inspecting the crumpled figure. "Hun-Came," said Mary Beth at last, shakily.

"The Lord of Death?" Maggie was still wheezing. "Maybe. I

151

was thinking of the other one. The one who knew that women find little creatures irresistible. Hummingbirds or kittens.''

"Oyew Achi? Well, it doesn't matter. He's the same, whatever name we put on him.''

"Whatever name . . . that's it!'' croaked Maggie excitedly. "God, I'm a dolt!''

"What?''

"D-O-L-T, dolt. I should've paid more attention to your Mayan wisdom, Swede. Damn!'' She was pulling off her belt. "Let's buckle old nameless here to that tree, in case he wakes up.''

Mary Beth took the belt and used it to lash his limp hands behind him, and then removed his belt and fastened his ankles together. She started to reach for the knife but Maggie said, "Uh-uh. Leave it. Fingerprints,'' and for the first time Mary Beth thought of evidence. They left the knife where it lay and dragged him away from it, adding Mary Beth's belt to the restraints and buckling his heavy form to a sturdy tree.

"Well,'' Maggie said hoarsely, "he won't go anywhere now for a while. Let's get the police.'' She gave Mary Beth a sidelong glance. "Guess maybe I'll spare your Ixil tapes after all.''

"Sporting of you,'' said Mary Beth dryly. "How's your side?'' There was blood spreading across Maggie's shirt now, and blood coming from her nose and split lip.

"No problem,'' said Maggie. "It'll make nice color pix for the jury.''

They climbed back up to their car. The dazed kitten blinked at them from the roadside grass, but couldn't get up. Mary Beth set it tenderly in the backseat.

"Got change?'' Maggie asked as she drove toward the cross-roads stores down the ramp road.

"For the phone? Sure.''

"I'll drop you at the first booth, then go back to keep an eye on things.''

"Okay.''

"Tell the police he needs an ambulance.''

"Okay.''

"And tell them to pick you up so you can show them exactly where we are. And tell them about the kitten. It acts drugged.''

"Okay.''

"Oh. One other thing,'' she added, pulling up at the public

152

phone outside a Quick Mart store. Mary Beth paused with the door open.

"Yeah?"

"Just . . . thanks."

"Oh, sure. Anytime." Their eyes met, smiling, and Mary Beth felt a clear, exultant, bubbling joy, like winning a race, like seeing the Cuchumatanes for the first time, like hearing Mozart. She said, "Guess I'm a swimmer too."

Then she got out and called the police.

His name turned out to be Henry Cooke, and he filled and serviced candy machines. He was married, with a three-year-old son, and a young brown-haired wife who was furious and indignant. She held the little boy on her knee as they all waited upstairs in police headquarters for their statements to be readied for signature. Henry Cooke himself had a concussion; he was conscious again but hazy, and police, doctors, and lawyers were checking his fitness for questioning. The kitten was being tested for drugs.

Maggie had been carefully photographed, even submitting to an artistically draped study of the gash along the side of her left ribs. Then she had scrubbed and Mary Beth had checked the wound prior to a doctor's inspection. She wasn't bleeding much anymore, but it still looked ugly. Her lip was swelling too, and the bruised nose and chin would be colorful the next few days.

The child suddenly wriggled loose and ran over to Maggie and began to hit her knee violently. She moved to grab his fist but thought better of it and waited stoically for the mother to arrive and take the boy's arm. She did it protectively, as though Maggie were the attacker.

"It's a frame," she said, intensely. "He didn't do no murders. Who's paying you?"

"No one, Mrs. Cooke. We're telling the truth."

"It's a frame. He was just making his rounds and you framed him."

"No, Mrs. Cooke. He really did it."

"He never used no knife. Just wait, they'll find your fingerprints on it!"

"No, Mrs. Cooke."

"And they won't pin those others on him either. Just wait. I'll swear he was at work all day Monday. And those other times too. We'll stop you."

153

"No, Mrs. Cooke. We're telling the truth."

"Mrs. Cooke?" An officer came over at last. "It'd be better if you didn't talk to the young ladies."

"They're trying to frame Hank!"

"That's what we're investigating now," he said soothingly. "Just sit back down over here."

"Well, it was Johnny here. I had to get him, didn't I?" She allowed herself to be led back across the room.

"She's got a lot of excuses for him," said Mary Beth.

"Yeah." Maggie was looking at them sadly. "I wish these guys didn't have families."

"Yeah." Mary Beth wondered briefly if Chipmunk-Fur had a family. Whether he treated his wife as he did other women. Obviously Henry Cooke treated his wife well enough to inspire this blind loyalty.

Eventually they were able to sign the statements and were allowed to go. Nick, holding a brown sack, was waiting in the broad entrance hall downstairs as they came down the steps. When she saw him, Maggie moaned, "Oh no! Not now! That's all I need! Why'd you tell him?"

Mary Beth was surprised. "Well, someone had to."

"You didn't have to tell him we were here. I would've lied."

"What would you have said?" Nick asked with some interest. He had come to the foot of the stairs to meet them, glancing at Maggie's battered face but not commenting. Her chin rose a fraction.

"I would've said that my ignition system had a short and that we'd see you some other time."

"So that I could continue a few more hours in blissful ignorance?"

"No. So that tonight's audience wouldn't be cheated out of a great performance."

He was surprised, a bit flattered and a bit rueful. "You always think of the greater good, don't you?"

"Of course, if it happens to be convenient."

"I'm an actor, Maggie. They won't be cheated."

She met his eyes an instant, grudgingly, then shrugged. "Yeah, I know. So Mary Beth is bang on target again. And I'm wrong." She crossed to the window and stood looking out at the dingy street, arms folded in front of her, stern and unhappy.

"Look," said Nick. "All Mary Beth said was that you helped

catch the Triangle Murderer. A tantalizing come-on. Could some-one please tell me what happened? Preferably in the next ten min-utes because I'm supposed to be putting on my nose already.''

"Read the papers," said Maggie grumpily. "There will be full and detailed accounts. Thanks to Mary Beth, it's news that's fit to print. No penetration.''

"Unless you count knives," said Mary Beth quietly. Alarm flashed in Nick's eyes and Maggie tossed her a look of disgust. He stepped wordlessly to Maggie's side, tucking the sack under his arm, and moved her arm carefully to inspect the sticky rip in the stained shirt and what could be seen of the wound underneath. She suffered his investigation without actively helping or hindering.

"Good as new in a couple of days," he said briefly.

Maggie relaxed a little. "Don't tell the jury. That's half our case.''

"I see: Woe to the hand that shed this costly blood.''

"Exactly." She subdued the ghost of merriment that sprang to her eyes and stared out the window again.

"Have you seen a doctor?''

"Next step. We're on our way to the university clinic now.''

"Fine. Now let's hear how it happened.''

Maggie continued to stare obstinately out the window, so Mary Beth said, "Well, Maggie spotted him on the ramp waving for help. He had a hurt kitten, and she realized that was the perfect way to make women stop to help. She made me hide behind the seat be-fore I figured out what was going on. Then she pulled off the road by his car and got out. He said he'd damaged his car swerving to avoid the kitten, and asked her to give him a lift to take the kitten to a vet. But she went to his car and got him to follow her.''

"How?''

"Started looking under his hood. He was furious.''

"And then?''

"Then she got him to pull the knife on her.''

"How clever of her. So wise so young, they say, do never live long. Where were you all this time?''

"On the backseat floor under her raincoat.''

"A pretty picture all around," said Maggie over her shoulder. "Entrapment and foolhardiness.''

"And then what happened?" Nick's tone was insistent.

Maggie swung around to face them, arms still crossed. "Not much more to tell. The entrapper and the entrapped pop into the

155

nearest bushes for a quick scuffle. The heroine pops out of the car with a wrench and dings the entrapped on the back of the head. The entrapper is saved, the entrapped is delivered to justice, the newspapers rejoice, the actor is late. End of story. Curtain.''

Mary Beth had been watching his warm brown eyes as he absorbed the curt story, concern and pride showing as he listened. She said, ''Nick, she's very tired.''

''And very hungry,'' he added. Maggie glared at them both and turned away abruptly to look out the window again; but when he reached into his brown sack and pulled out a thick sandwich and held it toward her, she hesitated only a moment before turning to take it and bite in.

Mary Beth accepted half a sandwich too, and for a minute they all stood around chewing thoughtfully. Then Nick said, ''Seems to me, Mary Beth, you deserve a medal.''

''Anyone would have helped.''

''Not if she'd gone through what you went through.''

''What I really wanted to do,'' she admitted, ''was roll up the windows and lock the doors.''

''But you had to save our headstrong friend here.''

''Well, I thought so at the time,'' said Mary Beth slowly. Maggie stopped chewing and looked at her warily over the top of her sandwich.

''What do you mean?'' asked Nick.

''I think now that she could have flipped him off whenever she wanted. She hadn't forgotten your lesson at Litchfield Park. She was waiting for something. For me.''

''My God, Swede. What a stupid idea,'' said Maggie, her mouth full, her eyes unsmiling.

''Well, you weren't having any real trouble keeping his knife away. And when you needed a breath I saw you distract him by moving your knee so that he eased off your mouth a second. And that picturesque cut on your ribs is right where you aimed it. Not him. He was aiming at your throat.''

''Your faith is touching,'' said Maggie. ''A half-hour lesson from Uncle Nick and you think I can overcome a sturdy sort who outweighs me by fifty pounds and has a knife.''

''I won't say it to a jury. Or even to a reporter.''

Maggie chewed for a moment, then said wearily, ''Damn you, Mary Beth. All that work for nothing.''

''No, not for nothing,'' said Mary Beth. ''You fooled me at the time, Maggie. I thought you needed help, and I helped. Now I know I can.''

Maggie finished her sandwich and licked her fingers. '''Course you can.'' She turned to Nick and added ungraciously, ''You're late. Why aren't you gone?''

''Because, Mademoiselle, I too want to explain a couple of basic truths to you.''

''Oh God. This is getting boring.''

''Right,'' said Mary Beth briskly. ''I'll wait in the car, Maggie.'' She dodged out the door and ran down to Maggie's car and slammed the door. Maggie, swearing, followed her out the door, but Nick caught up with her on the station steps and said something. She slowed, reluctantly. At the bottom of the steps they faced each other a moment, Maggie erect and defiant, Nick mild and unhurried despite his tardiness. Suddenly they both laughed at something he said, and Maggie, relaxed now, ran her fingers through her hair and then looked at him more gently. He smiled and took her right hand and, bowing in the correct theatrical fashion, carried her fingertips to his lips. Then he hurried to his car and drove away.

Maggie took a few slow steps toward her car but stayed on the sidewalk, looking after him. Mary Beth got out of the car again and joined her.

''What does he say?''

''That we are friends and therefore he won't leave me alone.''

''No matter how snotty you act.''

''Right. But he didn't put it so politely.''

His car had disappeared now but still they stood on the sidewalk looking at where they had last seen it. Maggie's fingertips strayed to her sore mouth. Mary Beth knew suddenly, certainly, what her subconscious had been trying to tell her, what her overtaxed emotions had twisted into fear of physical violation, when the threat was from another quarter altogether. She realized how very much her proud and independent friend had lost last weekend.

''I was late, wasn't I?'' she asked gently.

''What?''

''Tuesday night when I stupidly decided to protect you from Nick. I was a whole day late.''

Maggie snatched her traitorous fingers from her lips and stared at them an instant, then rubbed them roughly on her jeans. ''Goddamnit, you psychic Swede,'' she said angrily. ''You could let me have one secret!'' She slammed into the driver's seat and started the car, barely waiting for Mary Beth's door to close before plunging unsafely into the traffic.

"It's only fair," Mary Beth observed a bit breathlessly when she had caught her balance again. "You've been known to look through me on occasion."

Maggie didn't answer for a block or two. Finally she said, "It was just good old Uncle Nick. He didn't count. I stupidly let my guard down."

Mary Beth remembered that look of panic at the dance. "You're frightened," she said wonderingly. "Of yourself."

"Scared out of my skull. Another goddamn actor! God, it's the dumbest thing I ever did!"

"Oh, come off it."

"Well, second dumbest. Third. Third dumbest thing I ever did."

"Well, all right. That's more reasonable."

Maggie looked at her suspiciously, then smiled a little at herself. "Yeah. It's laughable. Well, there's a lot to do in this rotten world besides worry about dumb mistakes. I'll get over him. I'm getting a lot of practice at getting over things."

"Yeah. We all are."

Maggie nodded, and they sat with their own thoughts for a few miles. Then Mary Beth said, "Well, at least we did something for Jackie."

"What?" asked Maggie absently. She was still thinking of other things.

"What do you mean, what? We caught her murderer!"

"No, we didn't."

"No?"

"No, Mary Beth," said Maggie, as though surprised by her obtuseness. "Weren't you paying attention? He's not the one who murdered Jackie. Jackie's murderer is still free."

"Maggie, you're crazy! There can't be two like Henry Cooke!"

Maggie was passing a moving van and didn't answer for a moment. Then she said, "Yeah, you're right, Mary Beth. There can't be two like him. I just hadn't thought it all the way through."

XVII

1 Chee
(June 22, 1968)

After the night watchman had nodded at her and gone away, the building seemed desolate and ominous. Jane turned on Josh's radio and rotated the dial impatiently until she found some instrumental music coming out of Syracuse. That was better; she could concentrate a little now. It had been so hard to concentrate this week. And the building seemed so deserted tonight, which was distracting in itself. Every creak or click from the machines around her in the basement lab became portentous of dread. She reached in her bag and took a Valium.

The departmental approval had not really helped; she was more wound up than ever. The strain had just gone on for too long. She was really going to have to have a vacation soon. The finals for her summer school course would be tomorrow. Maybe Thursday or Friday she could leave. A beach somewhere, sea and sun. Could Roger go? She had lost track of his schedule completely. A long weekend, sea and sun and sex, that's what she needed.

She pulled her willful mind back to its task. She was sitting at Josh's desk in the equipment room, coding tapes for their new pilot study. This one did seem to be working better. Josh had rigged a double tape setup. The infant listened to a string of ba-ba-ba's until it began to habituate, then the experimental tape was switched on. The eight subjects they had had so far took amazingly different lengths of time to reach the same level of habituation; no wonder the original experiment had washed out. Well, they had the problem licked now, she was sure. Not all problems, of course. Some babies, for mysterious infant reasons, began to squall before anything much had happened. No respect for science. This younger generation. But at least she was gaining on the habituation problem with the new technique.

The building really was very quiet tonight.

She had a set of blanks for transcribing the raw data for each child from the long spools of graph paper with the red inked lines. For each change in syllables, she had to record the heart rate at point A before the change, and at point B after the change. Then she'd get the computer cards punched from the data sheets and have the computer figure out the differences in heart rate for each type of change. The computer would do the statistics too. Everything was carefully counterbalanced, of course, so that no one could say, "Professor Freeman neglected to consider the possibility that practice (or fatigue) caused the difference (or lack of difference) in response to variable X (or Y, or Z)." Tedious, but necessary. Each subject was unique, receiving one of the twenty-four possible orders of the four syllables on the tapes. Since there had only been eight so far, she naturally didn't have a complete balance yet. But things didn't look too bad at this point. She started on the sixth baby's data.

The radio announced that it was nine-forty-five and began to soft-sell an elegant restaurant in Syracuse, which no doubt played Muzaky background music itself. Jane took the commercial for an excuse to stretch and look around. Her own equipment, against the wall behind her, was neatly stowed, tapes filed, amplifier and polygraph battened down properly for the night. Her new tape recorder in its shiny metal cabinet sat on the table nearby. Above her, the extra shelves were finally being dismantled; the scaffold bars, like a jungle gym, were still there, but the chairman had finally located a dry room that was suitable for storing the unused equipment, and Josh had most of the machines and shelves moved out. In the back corner, someone was preparing new apparatus for a thermal perception experiment. Probably Milliken upstairs; he did environmental stuff. This would have to do with perception of radiant heat versus air temperature, Josh had told her. A crayoned sign on the circuit breaker box warned against turning on Breaker 14. The heating panels and blowers sat unattached in an untidy clump near the corner, and a brand-new control panel was already being wired up next to it. Science had certainly come a long way, she

160

thought wryly. In the old days you could just ask people if they were warm enough.

It was so hard to concentrate. The ad hoc committee, and Jackie Edwards's death, and the demands of WAR to do something, and summer school. Everything seemed to conspire against her poor little pilot study. Well, she'd just have to concentrate. She glowered at the neat columns and began again to fill them in from the next polygraph tape. But she had not gotten very far when there was a knock at the door. Well, that figured. Maybe two other people in the whole building, and one of them wanted to bother her.

"Come in," she said, and looked up. "My God, Maggie, what's happened to you?"

"You haven't listened to the news," said Maggie. "Some guy assaulted me today. But I'm okay." Her face was bruised and swollen.

"Are you really all right? Shouldn't you have a doctor look at you?"

"Already did. He says I'm ugly but okay. Look, I wanted to ask you a question. I just came from your office."

"Oh. Well, I had to work down here tonight . . ."

"I mean, I was in your office." Jane was surprised; she'd left it locked. Maggie explained, "I used my plastic ID card on the lock."

"Security in this place is rotten," said Jane dryly. "Well, okay, tell me what you want."

"What I want? Justice, I guess. I want to see Jackie's killer dead."

A violent sentiment, a calm voice. Jane looked at her closely, wondering if she had a concussion or something too. But then it was natural for her to be upset; she'd lost a close friend. Jane said soothingly, "Arrested, at least. We all want justice. It's a terrible thing, what that man is doing."

"Okay. Justice. I also want to carry out Jackie's last wish."

"Of course. Can I help?"

"Yes. She wanted you to sign something like this. I did the secretarial work for you."

Jane took the proffered paper. It was on departmental letterhead, addressed to the *Verbal Learning Quarterly*. It read: "I would like to make a final correction in the proofs for the article to be published in your September issue, 'Social Class Differences in the Acquisition of Negation.' The author should be listed as Sonia Michaelson, not as Jane Freeman. Thank you very much." There was space for Jane's signature.

Jane placed the letter carefully on Josh's desk.

Maggie said, "Before I typed this on your typewriter, I took the liberty of glancing through a couple of old files. You were at Graham College, an instructor, when Sonia did her honors project. And I looked at the drafts of the article itself. It's Sonia's work."

"Jackie said she had worked out the new statistics but hadn't told Sonia yet."

"True. If you'd given her another minute, she might have told you that I helped her work out the new statistics."

"Given her a minute?"

"Before your killed her."

Jane's mouth fell open. "Me? What are you talking about? Maggie, you're not well. Have you told anyone else about these insane suspicions?"

Maggie seemed amused. "What kind of question is that? Would you believe me if I said yes? Or no, for that matter?"

"You're right." Jane considered. "Actually I'd be more inclined to believe no. First, even you must realize it's an outrageous accusation. The police would not be convinced. Next, if you'd called the police you'd wait for them, not come here in person."

"Right on all counts, so far."

"After all, how can you seriously suggest that murder was committed for authorship of an esoteric article?"

"How can I suggest it? Well, I thought of how upset Jackie was after she saw the galley proofs for this article. And today a friend reminded me that the same thing may have different names. And I thought of how tough it is to get tenure. And I thought of your Volks being at the dealer in Schellsburg that Monday."

So she had worked that out. What a tiresome world this was. "The Triangle Murderer killed her, Maggie. But I suppose this is blackmail," Jane said wearily, reaching into her bag. "Well, you're absolutely right, I don't have time now to argue with the police. How much do you want?"

"For starts, I want you to sign that letter."

"Would fifty do?" Jane stood up with the bills in her hand. But Maggie bounded instantly onto the desk and up to the ceiling, grasping a scaffold pipe and hauling herself up smoothly to sit on it.

The letter-knife hidden behind the money in Jane's hand never had a chance to scratch her.

It had been so much easier with Jackie. It had happened so quickly and smoothly that even Jane hadn't quite realized it until it was done.

Not now. This one was tough. And there was no sense trying to bluff anymore. Jane put a chair on the desk and climbed onto it. But by the time she was within reach of the scaffold, Maggie had swung herself to another pipe and was now perched calmly on it. No way to catch her up there. A gymnast, someone had said. And in her airy element.

"I want to talk about a few things," Maggie said. "And for reasons that may become clear, I don't want any more marks on me just at the moment."

"Few people would." Jane abandoned her undignified roost, took Josh's pliers from his desk drawer, and walked across to the corner where the new heating panels sat.

Maggie shifted a little to keep her in sight. "Well, but there are considerations beyond the strictly hedonistic. Although it's true that I already hurt enough."

Jane, glancing up, saw that bright blood was seeping into Maggie's blouse under her arm. Swinging up onto the pipes must have opened the wound. This assault, then, had damaged more than her face. That was good news if they reached the hand-to-hand stage; Jane knew that otherwise she wouldn't have much of a chance. Maggie was fitter than she was, she remembered from the self-defense classes.

She made sure Circuit 14 was still off and, keeping a wary eye on the woman hovering above her, clipped off the new 240-volt outlet that Milliken's assistant had installed that day for the heating panels. She split the cable sheathing lengthwise for a couple of feet, separating out the three wires. Black was the hot lead, white was neutral, red was ground. She bared the thick copper of the black and white wires and wrapped the white one around one of the pipes that supported the scaffold Maggie was sitting on.

Maggie said, "Before you fry me, you really should know a few more facts."

"I'm always ready to learn," said Jane civilly. She attached a longer cable to the black wire and crossed back to the door, wondering why Maggie was not attempting to escape. Maybe she didn't think Jane was serious. Jane began to attach the cable to the scaffold leg nearest the door.

"Take a look at this," said Maggie. "The original has been mailed. I did make sure of that."

She dropped a paper, a carbon copy on onionskin, which fluttered to the floor. Jane kept the knife ready; Maggie could move fast, she knew. Maggie saw her hesitation and added, "Don't worry, I'm not coming down yet. I don't want more scars. And I do want you to read it."

Jane snatched the paper from the floor and backed up to guard the door again, although Maggie had not stirred. The radio shifted to a saccharine organ version of something by Verdi.

It was a copy of a letter from Maggie, addressed to Sonia Michaelson in New Jersey. "You probably already know that our friend Jackie Edwards was killed this June. Before she died, she had been intending to call your attention to the September issue of the *Verbal Learning Quarterly*. I understand that Professor Freeman of this university completed an article on your behalf. Jackie feared that since you had changed fields you might miss it, so I thought I would drop you a note."

That was all. September, thought Jane, that was all the time she had. Unless . . .

"If you sign that other letter," said Maggie, "there will be a very small prepublication scandal."

"Which will eliminate all possibility of tenure."

"Probably. If you don't sign, though, there will be a large postpublication scandal, including shocked retractions in the *VLQ*. Which will also eliminate tenure."

"True. But if I don't sign it, and you are dead, nothing will happen till September."

"When Sonia will see your name on the article and launch the large postpublication scandal. And that will put more than you under suspicion. It will also put your previous work under suspicion."

Her previous work. Damn, damn, damn. That had always been the problem. It went beyond this one article. She thought of the eight stacks of offprints in her office. Her other articles, her mind's children, would be discredited too, ignored. All those hours, all that struggle to get a professional reputation. To add a little to human knowledge. To claim her bit of immortality. She said, "It sounds as though I would be much better off without you and Sonia."

"Yes. If it weren't for the problem of bodies."

"You must know I've solved that problem."

"If you'll bear with me, I think you'll find there is now a major difficulty. Minor ones too. For example, two deaths from the same address, same car, are quite a coincidence."

"Though it's in character for you to go after killers," observed Jane acidly.

"Touché!" Maggie was amused. "But another problem will be my car. You aren't set up as well this time, with your own car waiting conveniently in the Schellsburg garage near the ramp. If you drive me there, how will you get back?"

"I'll think of something."

"I suppose you could use the South Syracuse ramp," Maggie mused. "The bus terminal is only a half-mile away."

Jane had not thought of the South Syracuse ramp. She said, "Thank you for the helpful hint."

"However, getting my car started may prove a problem this time."

"Oh?"

"It's parked across the lot. In gear, brakes on, doors locked. The key is under a bush in the hedge there. The distributor rotor is under another."

"You are cautious." Two hundred yards of hedge around that lot. Jackie, in contrast, had been parked just outside the loading door.

"But in any case, you'll want to wait till after ten."

"What does the time have to do with it?"

"The news will be on in a minute. You'll want to hear it."

"I will?"

"Definitely."

Jane leaned back against Josh's desk, knife still ready, and studied Maggie. Probably a play for time. Why? She was tired, Jane could see that. Bruised and pale, she'd probably lost blood already today. The slowly spreading red circle under her arm would not account for that much pallor. But she was still alert, still poised on her uncomfortable seat near the ceiling. An avenging angel, thought Jane suddenly, and then felt uneasy. Nonsense, she wasn't about to avenge anything.

But how the hell could she get that car away? The Volks couldn't tow that big old car. But it couldn't be left next to this building, a neon arrow for the police.

"Since you are determined that I should have all the facts," she said, deciding to show that she was aware of the situation, "shouldn't you speed things up a little? I don't have a lot of time, you know. Enough, but not a surplus. Night watchman, you know."

"I know." Maggie remained serene. "But you're more likely to believe it from the radio than from me."

Jane walked back across the room, uneasiness growing. She kept her eyes on Maggie, but was not surprised now that there was no attempt to escape. She had had several chances and had ignored them already. Clearly, she was staying. Why?

But Jane still had the upper hand. The circuit through the grid of pipes that made up the scaffold was complete now. All she had to do to kill her was flick the switch.

Of course, if she dropped down early, Jane would be in for a fight. An idea she didn't like at all.

The pseudo-Verdi ended and the news began. And there it was. First item. "Syracuse police announced today a major break in the Triangle Murders case. A Syracuse man, Henry Cooke, has been arrested after an attack on two State University students, Mary Beth Nelson and Margaret Ryan. The women escaped with minor injuries. Detectives would not comment on how many of the crimes Cooke will be charged with. Cooke is a . . ."

Jane lurched across the room and snapped off the radio and leaned dizzily onto the desk.

Maggie said, "Cooke is Caucasian, drives a gray Chevrolet, and uses a hurt kitten as a lure for soft-hearted women. And Jackie, of all people, would never have stopped to help a man on a highway ramp near Syracuse."

Jane commanded her head to stop spinning. She said unsteadily, "You stopped for him."

"Well, I'm not Jackie, I'm me. As you yourself just pointed out, it's in character for me."

"And your . . . existing . . . wounds have probably been recorded by the police. I see."

"I thought you'd see. The latest in modern forensic technology has surrounded me all afternoon. Every scratch and pimple has been recorded and declared nonfatal. There is even a second record, made just an hour ago, by an excited university clinic intern

166

who has visions of becoming a hero with his evidence when Cooke's trial rolls around.''

Jane's mind checked off the implications. She could not get rid of the body as she had before. Or the car. She could not even count on the usual delay that tended to follow the disappearance of a student. Students generally expected their friends to behave erratically from time to time, and seldom reported disappearances immediately. Jackie had not been reported missing. But Maggie was a temporary celebrity now. Her car was disabled in the parking lot of this building. If she disappeared, or if her body were found, there would be a full inquiry. Starting with people who were in this building tonight.

"You could turn on the barbecue here," Maggie said helpfully, "but you'd still have to put me somewhere. You wouldn't want me found in your lab."

"And you wouldn't wait up there for it anyway. I was only wiring it up to encourage you to come down."

"A giant cattle prod. I see. Still, I imagine that these new facts make you more reluctant to knife me."

"Correct. But more eager than ever to make you disappear."

"Naturally. Still, what are your options now? You can't just let me go, of course. You'll end up jailed."

Jail. A little thick-walled room. A closed door. Jane said, "Of course." What the hell did Maggie want?

"If you manage to kill me, however, you'll also end up in jail. Probably soon, since the police are currently taking an interest in me and my car. But if you're lucky, perhaps not until September, if they need Sonia's evidence to inspire them to complete insight about who in this building might want me dead."

Jane had forgotten about Sonia. The foolish vision she had had, of overpowering Maggie somehow (how?) and getting her to the gorge and pushing her in, evaporated. No way to overpower her in the first place, no solution even if she did.

Jail if she let her go. Jail if she killed her somehow.

Her work discredited in any case.

Also discredited if Sonia Michaelson reported who had written the article. And the difficulties of killing Maggie were doubled in the case of Sonia, who would have to be located somehow and headed off before she could mention the letter to anyone. God, thought Jane, I don't even remember what Sonia looks like.

And then there was Roger. What would it do to his career? She could almost hear his boss now. "Roger, I understand that you . . . ahem . . . cohabited for four years with a murderess. We must . . . terminate our business association, I'm sure you will understand."

She looked at Maggie tiredly. "I didn't mean to," she said. "It was just an impulse."

"The article or the murder?"

"Both. I reworked Sonia's material with the correct statistical treatment back at Graham College the summer after she did it. I didn't direct her work, you see; I would have told her to analyze it correctly. I was just the outside reader. But it intrigued me enough to reanalyze it. But before I could tell her, she moved into another field at another university, and then I was appointed here, and I forgot about it until tenure started breathing down my neck."

"And there it was in your files, ready to ship off."

"Yes."

"And Sonia would never see it. So it was just bad luck that a friend of Sonia's happened by."

"It was already mailed, and even accepted."

"And you couldn't bear a scandal. Because of tenure, and because it would make your other work suspect."

"And it's all important work," said Jane with fierce maternal pride.

"I know it is. We're agreed on that." She seemed to understand.

"I've never fudged data. It's rock-solid."

"I know. If I thought the work was sloppy you wouldn't have this chance tonight. Listen, you said Jackie was an impulse too."

"She came here Monday. Said she wanted to talk privately."

"Two-thirty in the lab?"

"Yes. Josh was gone, organizing the new storage room. And she asked me to do the same thing you did, notify the journal. I just remember thinking, I wish she was dead. And suddenly she was."

Maggie nodded sadly. "I see."

"But then everything fell out so neatly. The loading door over there was unlocked for Josh. I had her car and keys, and my own car was waiting to be picked up near Syracuse. All I had to do was . . ." She stopped abruptly.

"Yes. I saw it. I had to identify her." Maggie's voice was cold, and suddenly Jane was forced to face it, and to realize what she had done. And to realize what she had been about to do tonight. She hid her face. Not an Innocent Bystander after all.

168

"It wasn't me," she said desperately. "Not really. It's the strain."

Maggie did not comment for a moment, just observed from her airy seat. Then she said, "Sign the letter."

"Why the hell should I?" said Jane, trying to collect her courage. "I'm just deciding whether I should try to take you down with me or not. Why should I sign that letter for you?"

"Not for me. For you. For the good work you've done."

"When you or Sonia start talking, the good work is suspect. Kaput."

"Look, work it out, okay? Sonia won't start anything if she sees her own name on the article."

"True." Jane thought for a minute. "I might even get a thank-you note, don't you think? No tenure, but a thank-you note. She can send it to the jail." She almost giggled.

"Tenure, I think, is out," said Maggie, and brought her back from the edge of hysteria.

Okay. No tenure, she was right. No tenure no matter what she did. And also jail, no matter what she did. And losing Roger. And worst of all, her work was doomed. No matter what she did. So why bother anymore?

She dropped the knife into her bag and unwrapped the wire slowly from the pipe next to the door, and coiled the cable again as she crossed the room. Then she began to unwind the white wire from the other pipe. Her mind stumbled about, searching for an escape. Jail . . . or jail? Discredited work . . . or discredited work? Maggie watched her sadly from above.

"I still don't understand why you didn't just tell the police," Jane asked finally. "Why are you here?"

"Because I want to finish what Jackie started. She wanted Sonia to get credit for her work."

"Yes."

"But she did not want to destroy the value of what you've accomplished yourself. Why else would she have kept quiet when she saw those galleys at the WAR meeting?"

"So you noticed that too."

"I'm afraid she didn't fully appreciate the tenure problem, though. My dad's a professor; I did."

There was a pause.

Jane said, "You explained that if I signed the letter, Sonia would have no reason to start a process that would discredit my work. You didn't explain what would keep *you* quiet.''

"Oh, but I did.''

There was another pause.

"You said you wanted justice,'' said Jane slowly.

"Yes.''

Maggie waited.

"You seem to be suggesting that under certain conditions you would not reveal the circumstance of Jackie's death.'' She met Maggie's eyes and saw that she was right.

Maggie said, "It's your choice, of course. But I don't see much sense in giving academic women a bad name. Most of us play by the rules. And my buddy Henry Cooke might as well be tried for nine deaths as eight. Under certain conditions, as you say.''

Jane went to the desk and stared at the letter. She could, perhaps, save her good work. Limit the damages to this one mistake, let the rest live on. And she might save Roger from the stigma of criminal association. But could she really trust Maggie to keep silent? She glanced up again. The blue gaze was implacable. Justice, she had said. That would have to do.

She signed the letter.

She scribbled a note on an index card too. "Dear Roger, This pressure to get tenure is just too much for me. I love you.''

Then she put on her lab coat and picked up the electrolytic salve and crossed back to finish unwinding the white wire from the corner pipe. She fastened it to the metal cabinet of her own unplugged tape recorder, because that would look more realistic. The black wire, the one that would be charged, bent up cobralike a foot away. "The night watchman,'' she said, "will be back here about ten-thirty-five.''

"Okay,'' said Maggie. "The letters and I will be gone.'' She added with sober respect, "I was thinking of overdosing on Valium. You're right, this is a lot better.''

Jane rubbed the electrolytic salve carefully into her skin and wrapped the shining copper end of the black wire firmly around her right wrist under her watchband, so that it wouldn't slip as she moved. Then she lifted the wired recorder cabinet and set it on her left hand, its weight heavy and metallic on her palm. "Well,'' she said to Maggie, "cheers.'' And then, after only the smallest of hesitations, she flicked on Circuit 14.

EPILOGUE

3 Hunaapu
(September 23, 1968)

Mary Beth took a last sniff of the crisp September evening air. A good day, Hunaapu again. She went into the brightly lit old house, unlocked the office door, and plunked her Ixil materials down on the desk. Professor Greene was pleased with her thesis so far and she hoped to get something done tonight on Chapter Six.

The house was on the edge of campus behind the chapel, and belonged officially to the Methodists. The chaplain had been very eager to help, something to do with the church in society. "Splendid, splendid!" he had enthused. "We had a draft counseling group in that room but they moved into larger quarters. Now we have the English classes for foreign students on the second floor, and the Word of the World Press, and of course our own counseling program. We'd love to have you too."

"We can pay for our own phone and supplies, of course," said Mary Beth. The Rape Crisis Line had received one of the first grants from the Jane Freeman Memorial Fund for Women, organized by her grieving, grateful students.

Now Mary Beth checked the message pad. Only two notes. A radio station in Syracuse wanted to interview someone in their group; and Lila, a recent victim, had called but said she would ring again about 10 p.m. Lila was a waitress whose boyfriend, initially stunned, had found his tongue and now spent his time raging at her for being a whore; he'd half-convinced her that in fact the rape was really her fault.

A cluster of Japanese and Indian students, chattering incomprehensibly, came into the hall and started up the stairs to class. Mary Beth waited for them to pass, then called the radio station and arranged for an interview over the weekend. She was getting to be very good at interviews. Henry Cooke's trial had given them lots of practice. It had been odd to be part of the bloody fabric of news programs. Vietnam, or the Chicago Democratic Convention police riots, or the assassination of U.S. Ambassador Mein in Guatemala might be featured, and then Mary Beth and Maggie would be telling their story.

Sue was delighted. "I told you!" she exclaimed. "All you have to do is fight back and they'll pay attention!"

"Today Henry Cooke, tomorrow the world," said Maggie, unimpressed.

One of Nick's letters contained a mock review of their appearance on a national news program. The review claimed that "The heroine, M. B. Nelson, turned in a competent and appealing performance," but that "acting honors belong to M. Ryan for an amazingly convincing impersonation of an innocent auto mechanic lured unwittingly into danger." Maggie had smiled at it, crumpled it into a wastebasket, and run out to split wood.

Mary Beth was just reaching out to take the cover from the typewriter that the Methodists had scrounged for them when there was a hesitant knock on the open door.

She looked up and wondered how long he had been standing there—his dark eyes worried, a tall, shy, loosely built young man in a checked shirt and jeans. He shifted his books to his other hand. *Applied Calculus. Stress in Metals.* An engineer.

"Can I help you find something?" she asked.

"This is the rape counseling office?"

"Yes."

"I'm Craig Barnett."

"Hello. Mary Beth Nelson."

He shifted his books nervously again. The third book, oddly, was in Spanish. The plays of García Lorca. He said, "I, um, wanted to help."

Mary Beth stood up and smiled politely. "Well, thank you, Craig. But we've found that generally women prefer to talk to other women about it." Another well-meaning kook. Not as pushy as some, though. Painfully shy, really.

He stood there stiffly, a little frightened of her, but stubborn.

"Yes, but I mean the men," he said. "I mean . . . Look, the thing is, my sister was raped."

"I see." But she didn't, quite.

"She was at the laundromat. Same as every week. And this guy forced her."

"Do you want us to talk to her?"

"No, no. This was a couple of years ago in New Jersey. She's doing better now. But the thing is, I was home then. It was just before I had to leave for Central America for the Peace Corps. And she came running straight from the laundromat to my mom and me, and told us what happened."

"Yes."

"And I was furious. I've never been so angry in my life." His lips tightened with the remembered agony of rage and helplessness. Mary Beth suddenly felt very motherly toward him. He continued, "I wanted to kill that guy, really. And I'm a sort of peaceful person."

"That's the natural way to feel."

"Yes, but you see, I was so helpless. There wasn't a damn thing I could do."

"Yes."

"And so what I did was, I yelled at my sister—I told her that she was a damn fool for doing the laundry alone. I asked her why she hadn't kicked him in the balls."

"She probably tried."

He hurried to explain. "I was so upset, I accused her anyway. And worse. I asked her how she could disgrace the family like that. How she could do something like that to me."

Mary Beth sat down suddenly on the edge of the desk. "My God," she said.

"Yes, I know. Later my sister told me that was almost as bad as the rape. When I said those things to her."

"Yes, I see," she said weakly.

"But it was because I felt so helpless, you know? And so angry."

"Yes, I see." Oh God, I see, I see.

He was only awkward on the surface, she found. The bashful dark eyes took in a lot. He said, "Somebody said that kind of stuff to you too."

"Yes. And I didn't know why till this minute. I was dumb, I guess." Nick had said it too, hadn't he? Your heart plays tricks on

173

you, you start seeing yourself as the victim. Poor Tip. She added, "It's obvious, isn't it?"

"Not really. My sister said the problem was being so upset herself. Otherwise she might have understood. As it was, she said if there had been any way to divorce a brother, she would have."

"Yes."

"And it took me a while to figure it out too. Then I was really ashamed of myself."

"Yes." Had Tip figured it out? No, he would have told her. Unless he was ashamed too. Well, it was too late now. But the hard knot of bewildered anger and hurt she had felt toward him was dissolving.

Craig said, "I thought maybe I could help people, because it happened to me too. You know, parents and brothers and husbands. Keep them from hurting people more, when they're really desperate to help."

She was silent a moment, looking at the angular, earnest young man who had brought her such an unlikely and unexpected gift. Then she said, "There's someone I want you to talk to tonight. She'll be calling about ten o'clock. Her boyfriend is telling her it was her fault."

"Yeah, sure. I can stay awhile. Poor woman."

"Poor boyfriend too," said Mary Beth. She sat down in her chair again. "Have a seat, Craig. We definitely need you. Let me give you the ground rules our counselors have worked out."

"Great!" The dark eyes twinkled when he smiled. She was glad that she wasn't making him nervous anymore. It must have taken courage to confess what he had just confessed. He leaned forward in his chair and asked eagerly, "You really think I can help people?"

"I really do, Craig." She smiled at him. "You've helped your first already."

CHARLOTTE MACLEOD

"Suspense reigns supreme"   <u>Booklist</u>

THE BILBAO LOOKING GLASS   67454-8/$2.95 US/$3.75 Can

Sleuth Sarah Kelling and her friend, art detective Max Bittersohn are on vacation at her family estate on the Massachusetts coast, when a nasty string of robberies, arson and murders send Sarah off on the trail of a mystery with danger a little to close for comfort.

WRACK AND RUNE   61911-3/$2.95 US/$3.75 Can

When a hired hand "accidentally" dies by quicklime, the local townsfolk blame an allegedly cursed Viking runestone. But when Professor Peter Shandy is called to the scene, he's sure it's murder. His list of suspects—all with possible motives—includes a sharp-eyed antique dealer, a disreputable realtor, and a gaggle of kin thirsty for the farm's sale!

SOMETHING THE CAT DRAGGED IN   69096-9/$3.25

The Balaclavian Society only recruited the town's snobs, but was something rotten in the upper crust? Professor Peter Shandy suspects that someone has stooped low enough to murder. And with the help of Police Chief Fred Ottermole and Edmund, Betsy Lomax's feckless feline, he's out to collect the clues that will catch a killer.

Also by Charlotte MacLeod:
THE PALACE GUARD   59857-4/$2.95 US/$3.75 Can
THE WITHDRAWING ROOM   56473-4/$2.95 US/$3.75 Can
LUCK RUNS OUT   54171-8/$2.95 US/$3.75 Can
THE FAMILY VAULT   49080-3/$2.95 US/$3.75 Can
REST YOU MERRY   47530-8/$2.95 US/$3.95 Can

AVON PAPERBACKS